PRECIOUS ELEMENTS

by
JENNIFER
DETLEFSEN

BOOK ONE

CONTENTS

THE FIND

   Sarah's heart started pounding. She peered closer at the instrument in front of her, yes, the scanner had picked up something. She quickly switched the air mobile into hover position and checked the reading. The scanner had detected an object on the ground of large proportion five kilometres ahead. But Sarah would have to get closer for the scanner to give a better indication of the size and shape of the object. David Spencer, her boss at the Earth Intelligence Agency, EIA, had said this may be a dangerous mission since they were dealing with unpredictable aliens from other planets so she was to keep out of sight. Also they did not want the intruders to know that they'd been discovered and were being observed.

   She'd now have to leave the hovercraft and continue on foot. She needed to keep the craft a reasonable distance away because the aliens would probably have detection equipment of their own operating. She thought five kilometres would be a safe distance to avoid detection. And if there were any guards stationed they'd be looking for air-mobiles or zoom-cars, they would never expect anyone to be out here in the heat of the desert on foot. She asked the computer a question. "Exterior temperature is forty five degrees centigrade," the computer answered. She looked around and could almost see the searing heat in the air. She wasn't thrilled about the prospect of getting out of the cool car. She landed and asked another, "Distance five point two kilometres, time in human steps approximately one hour," the computer obliged. So a two hour round trip, she thought. She picked up her backpack and said

"Open door." The window slid up into the roof and the side doors slid back into the body of the car.

"Close and cloak," she said as she got out and the hover became invisible. She took out a device from her backpack and pressed the button that made everything within a meter of herself invisible to any heat or movement detector. And so she set off on her walk to the location that her hand held scanner indicated. It showed that the large objects were bigger than a man and they were mobile, so she was pretty sure they were some kind of machinery. Someone was doing something out here in the middle of the Arabian desert and she was going to find out what it was.

  Sarah looked around her but it seemed all the scenery looked the same. She was in a desert, a barren wasteland, a sandy landscape of hills stretching for miles in every direction. Here and there cacti that had

grown to enormous sizes dotted the scene with their inviting bright red blossoms waiting to capture their next meal. Some plants had evolved into carnivorous organisms, able to eat large insects and small reptiles that emerged when the heat of the day had mellowed. Flesh eating plants were not the only thing that were unusual in the Earth's' desert. Random miniature fires that would start in a dry bush would take a life of their own and be whipped up into a small cyclonic wind, travelling for minutes burning everything in their path until extinguishing themselves as quickly as they had started.

  "What could Bosworth and his men be looking for?," she thought. Surely there couldn't be anything of value out here in the desert. But if Earth Intelligence were right they'd found something worth travelling solar systems for and spending a huge amount of international exchange over.

Sarah glanced at her watch. She'd been walking now for only fifteen minutes but the heat seemed oppressive. She knew she couldn't last another forty five minutes of walking without some help. She took two pills out of her bag and popped them in her mouth. They tasted sweet like candy but they weren't made of sugar. The first was a temperature regulating pill that would reduce her bodies' temperature to a normal level and keep it there for twenty four hours, and the second was a hydrator to preserve her sodium and water levels. But she took a big gulp of water anyway, from the small bottle she carried. She wanted to feel the cold water on her lips and in her mouth, a relief from the dry parched atmosphere.

She decided to sit down and rest until the tablets started working. Again she put her hand in her bag and took out a little square piece of shiny material. She gave it a quick shake and it opened up into a sun reflecting shelter. She sat down and took a sip of water and thought about what lay ahead. Her job was simply to confirm that there was actually mining going on in the desert, the rest was up to El. At the moment all the information about Bosworth was ambiguous and unconfirmed, he was a new player in the power systems of the planets and no one seemed to know how he had made his fortune or where he'd come from but his means were rumoured to be questionable. He was ostentatious and had quickly become well known and the fact that he would make an appearance on Earth, a relatively poor country with limited resources, was troubling. Sarah had seen pictures of him and although he was supposed to be of human ancestry she found him decidedly ugly. He was a big man, larger than the average human man, with muscly arms and big fingers. He wore his jet black hair cropped short, so that it struck straight up out of his head, making his pointy nose more prominent. His eyes were small and squinted as if he were perpetually looking into the sun, his mouth was pursed tightly shut but he always wore a self satisfied smirk on his face and Sarah had never seen him smiling in any of his images. He wore the finest of material in his suits and liked to adorn himself with gold trinkets, extravagantly hanging thick chains around his bulky neck, bracelets on his wrists and rings of various stones on each of his twelve fingers. His trademark was the crystal studded gold belt he wore hanging below his big belly. In all the images Sarah had seen of him he always wore his hand over the laser gun he had strapped to the belt, the permit only bestowed upon proven leaders of a planet. She hoped that she never had to meet him and abruptly felt a slight apprehension about her assignment.

She felt revived again after her short rest and resumed walking. She checked the miniature compass she carried containing the direction coordinates, making sure the alarm was switched on, which would beep if she strayed off course. That done, she looked around as she strode on.

The silent desert was a uniform yellow, an endless merging of golden sand and brilliant blue sky. The huge sun hung suspended, a great pendulum pouring out heat with a vengeance. She let her mind wander, trying not to dwell on the heat, thinking of all that had happened over the last few years. Not that long ago her life had been very ordinary, living day by day like everyone else did. Working as an animal keeper in one of the elite zoos in the city, she'd been supporting herself after her parents and younger brother left to find work in another solar system. Nervous though she'd been to be left alone, she'd decided to stay behind as well paid secure jobs were difficult to find. She still had her close friends who were like a second family to her and though she missed her real family, she soon forgot her loneliness. She was generally happy with her life but sometimes she felt there was something missing. Her friends told her she needed a man in her life, but no one she'd met had been special. Then all of a

sudden strange things had started happening. It began in her dreams, where she repeatedly dreamed of two exotic looking cats, dark cats with bright shining green eyes, urging her to follow them, to run with them, to
play with them. They were always the same two cats and they seemed to want to befriend her. After a while the dreams stopped and she forgot about them. But then she started having visions of the cats during the day, at any time. She would be doing ordinary things like working, eating or talking to her friends and they would come on suddenly without warning. At first she didn't think her experiences were important and she shrugged them off as being unusual but nothing significant.

Then one day she was sitting at breakfast watching the local system news when she gasped. In one of the reports was a picture of the two cats that she'd been having the visions of. The headline above the picture read 'Rare Cats Missing – Reward'. She touched the screen of the receiver and the story reported in more detail. Sarah looked intently at the screen as it said that two expensive and rare species of intelligent felines had been imported into a neighbouring planet by a rich merchant but had mysteriously disappeared while being quarantined. There was also a number to contact for anyone with any information. Sarah mused over the report for a few days before deciding to call the number. She wasn't sure if she could say exactly where the cats were, but she may be able to recognise their surroundings in her next vision. If there was one.

Sarah had now been walking for about forty minutes and knew she must be getting close. She started to take more notice of her surroundings and looked for any indications of activity. But the terrain she was now covering had emerged into small hills and she could not see beyond the latest one she was walking over. A touch of nausea came over her and she knew she was about to see a vision of the cats. She sat down on the soft sand so that it wouldn't have too much effect on her. She felt shaking and heard a rattling noise. There were steel bars in front of her eyes and knew that the cats were in a small cage being transported. She could feel them huddled together, frightened, as was the constant feeling they had these days.

She heard a loud noise and the vision was broken. She climbed to the top of the hill she was on and looked down at the changed scenery. In front of her was an army of activity, trucks, tractors, large drills boring down into the red sand of the earth.

She had found what she was looking for. There were no construction signs, fences or barriers spread around the site, no company logo showing who they were; the people responsible were obviously not expecting any company. She took a plethora of pictures and headed back towards her car.

PLANET ZENAR

Planet Zenar was a strikingly beautiful planet. Surrounded by five suns the atmosphere was tainted by rich hues of gold. The sun-kissed sandy hillsides gave way to warm golden skies on the horizon, but the vast orange ocean which covered half the planet kept the temperature at a mild thirty degrees centigrade. It was thought that the planet was at one time covered in ice, perhaps before a single sun exploded, and broke up into four other pieces. The bottom of the ocean had been measured to be much cooler than the surface, and it was here, ten kilometres below, that a very rare and powerful mineral had been discovered by the planets inhabitants. Krystal Gold was a golden toned, clear crystal with an electrical charge of enormous power in its elements. It transferred easily and at high speed between mediums and therefore could be used for endless applications. And all of a sudden it revolutionized the lives of firstly the people on its own planet and then the civilizations of others, as space travel became instantaneous for closer solar systems and reduced travelling further to mere days, rather than months or years. Of course Zenar wasn't the only planet to have found deposits of Krystal Gold but it was one of only a few. It transformed the lives of a humble race of people and catapulted them into the modern world.

The dark skinned Zenar people were an ancient civilization that had in the past been governed by rituals and superstitions pertaining to the sun-god they named 'Ra', who travelled by boat across the vast sea to the underworld on the other side.

But with space travel the Zenar society had to grow up quickly and learn to to trade in the Krystal and do business with all kinds of different races of people. At first they traded in the crude stone and sold to the wholesalers who made money manufacturing the stone into a form that could be used to transfer energy, but the Zenarians soon learned to manufacture it themselves and built vast factories to produce the usable form of the Krystal and earn more profits for themselves. As news travelled of a new planet that had discovered Krystal, races from further afield came to deal with the planet Zenar and the mild mannered citizens who possessed it. For a while they traded without any problems but it was inevitable that eventually someone would try to take advantage of the innocent and ignorant way in which the Zenarian people looked on the world. They came in the form of the Giants. A primitive race from a

primeval planet that had been plundered and decimated of its resources by its own inhabitants over the centuries, the giants had become brutes of the civilized world due to their sheer size, using it to kill and maim others, so that many had been killed themselves or jailed on various planets and restricted from entering others. This led to the beginning of their demise, and because of this some scientists believed they were a dying race, unable to fully feed and clothe their kindred. So they spread out forming small colonies on other planets who would accept them. The giants were becoming more desperate but of all races found the Zenarian people a kind and generous host, allowing the giants to live on the planet in ever increasing numbers. They endeared themselves to their generous keepers, but after decades of living on the planet, the giants forgot the gratitude their forbears had settled with, and decided that they also would like to reap the benefits that the Zenarian people enjoyed from their rich mines of precious stone. For the nation had grown into an extravagant and resplendent society, with the genteel and noble monarchy building magnificent palaces and palatial residences for their citizens to live in, and the race had become a cultured and cultivated race. The Zenarian monarchy, who controlled every aspect of the planets workings, were at first surprised at any request by the giants to gain any benefit from their revenue, and then became affronted and insulted when the giants persisted. After all the giants did no work at all but lived solely off the generosity of their hosts. But after being denied any additional endowment, the giants revolted in one huge show of force against their hosts, rounding up the helpless individuals into old underground caves and holding them as prisoners, while to the outside world business went on as usual. The giants threatened to kill the royal family if their subjects did not agree to continue living as normal and the people were so loyal to the ruling monarchy that they were horrified at the thought of having them put to death. They therefore helplessly agreed to the giants demands. At that time travel to and from planet Zenar was open to anyone but the giants forced the reigning king, King Raoul, to make an announcement that entrance into the planet was henceforth prohibited.

The giants then forced the Zenarians to be their servants, cooking and cleaning for them, and mining the precious crystal for them.

Prince Adabi's grandfather, King Raoul, was a young man at that time and head of the monarchy that had ruled over their people for centuries. He
had been crowned king very young when his father had been killed in an accident involving his travel ship. It had crashed into its destination planet and no one on the royal ship had survived. He had learned to rule from a young age and his own tragedy had made him a sympathetic and fair ruler.

Now he had a young son of his own and looked forward to the initiation ceremony that would crown his young boy a

Prince at age ten. His people were a quiet gentle race, and warmed by the heat of their suns enjoyed a peaceful existence. They learned that they had a longer life span than peoples from other planets and also found that when they left their planet they did not feel as healthy or strong as when they were at home. So they tended to remain amongst themselves and ignorant of the outside world. They paid high respect to the governing ruling family and their general goodwill was well known.

So it was quite a shock when they found that the hospitality that they had extended towards the giants was turned against them. It took them years before King Raoul rallied his people and developed a plan to rid the planet of the invading giants forever. For every time he looked upon his son, Raoul knew he could not crown him a prince as a slave. And the giants turned out to be a nasty, brutish race, taken to unnecessary cruelty and so instilled a hatred amongst their captives never experienced before.

But with the increased culture of their planet came increased knowledge also, and, as opposed to the large clumsy giants, the Zenarians were an intelligent race, their scientists being amongst the best known in the worlds. After years of imprisonment and secret heated meetings, King Raoul put his top chemists to work to find a poison to eradicate their captors; he felt he had no other choice. He would never again be the ruler who allowed his people to become powerless and slaves to another race. And he would not put the fate of his planet and his people in the hands of the governing bodies of the solar systems. He did not trust the outside world any longer, they had betrayed them; and he knew if he did so his resources would again be plundered. No, they would do it themselves, in secret, just as the invading giants had chosen to destroy them, in secret. The world would never find out what had transpired on their precious land.

They needed to find a substance that could be placed in food that was colourless, odourless and tasteless, and also that could be found in abundance on the planet. The scientists knew of such a toxin. There was a common yellow fungi that grew along the shoreline, and food that was stored nearby was commonly susceptible to the associated mould, particularly corn and peanuts. The name of it was Aspergillus flavus that produced a poison that was undetectable. It caused immunosuppression and liver cancer that eventually resulted in death.

King Raoul had his answer and his revenge. His people were secretly told not to eat any peanuts or corn and the scientists introduced the poison into those foods. It was a slow and painful death for the giants but the Zenarians had no mercy after they'd lost their freedom and their dignity. Eventually all the giants were eradicated from the planet and no more entry was permitted from any other nationality.

The Zenar people learnt a painful lesson from this horrific experience in their past, and every year they held a tribal ceremony to remind them of how horrendous it had been, and so that future generations would never forget how they nearly lost their beautiful planet and the resources it contained.

The planet thereafter was virtually cut off from the outside world for centuries and entry was forbidden except by royal decree. But the rare crystal was in high demand amongst other planets, so trading channels again increased over time. Zenar became one of the richest planets in all solar systems and the opulent golden castles they built to live in had every luxury imaginable. The people wanted for nothing and resumed their quiet relaxed and happy existence.

And in more recent years the king in his old age, Adabi's father, had begun to relax the impenetrable security his own father, the famous King Raoul had established, and encouraged his son to see more of the outside world.

But it was to be a regretful decision.

VISIONS

"Hello?"

"Yes what can I do for ya ma'am?"

"Ah, I wanted to talk to someone about those cats that were kidnapped, you know the ones on the news?"

"Yep miss, what did you want to know?"

"Well I might know something about them actually."

" Yeah like what?"

"Oh well do I just tell you over the phone or do I need to see someone?"

" Up to you ma'am, you can tell me now or come in and talk to someone but we're pretty busy at the moment, have you seen them or what?"

"Ah not exactly, I've seen them in my dreams." Sarah knew as soon as she'd said those words that they sounded stupid.

"In your dreams, you say?", smirked the officer on the other end of the phone.

"Well, they're visions actually, I can see what's happening to them, I sort of go into a daze and I can see what they see, you know?"

"Ok and what do they see miss?" She could hear that his voice was becoming impatient and she didn't know what to say to convince him.

"Well today I saw them just playing with each other as cats do, you know, wrestling and climbing up trees and they have big green piercing eyes....."

"Now look here Miss, I have a lot of real work to do so I suggest you keep this line clear now, ya got that Miss?!" And the line went dead.

Sarah felt like a fool and thought she better keep her visions to herself from now on.

The visions had started quite innocently like the last one, with the cats happy in their environment, playing and stretching, scratching their sharp claws into trees, the things that all cats like doing. Sarah would be working or drinking coffee with her friends when she'd feel a strange sensation coming over her, and slowly blackness would close in. At first she'd fall over wherever she was and her friends would quickly catch her but she wasn't aware of them doing it. But after a few times she began to recognise the odd dizzy feeling in her head when one of the visions were about to start and she'd excuse herself from whatever she was doing and find a quiet place to sit down until they passed. She was able to keep the visions to herself this way as well, as her friends had become worried something was wrong with her, and when the frequency of the visions increased it started affecting her work. She'd been called into her managers' office but she had managed to talk her way out of any trouble by feigning migraines.

But now she could tell when a vision was about to start and she'd slink away to somewhere she could be alone, even if it was just the nearest public lavatory.

At first Sarah could not feel anything the cats' felt – she was only an observer. She could see them play and eat, and sometimes it seemed like they were looking at her, but she became instantly enamoured by them, they were so gentle in their nature, and elegant in their movements. She could not help but admire their graceful demeanour and felt privileged to observe them. They knew that she was there watching but did not seem to mind her intrusion and she was fascinated.

They were larger than the feline earth cat, they reminded her more of the cheetah that was confined in one of the reserves in Africa, but not quite as lean and much more beautiful. But of course these animal were not wild, she realized, they were pets and after a few visions she would recognise the place they lived. Not only that but they were very intelligent cats, and as time wore on she became more in tune to them, knowing when she needed to see what they were seeing, and eventually feeling their feelings and thinking their thoughts.

One day she was sitting on her balcony alone in her apartment enjoying one of the visions. She could now tune in and out of their lives at will, and she knew that they did the same, at times she would suddenly become aware that the cats were with her, watching what she was doing. Sometimes it annoyed her and she'd started practising blocking them out but when they resisted her will she thought it was funny and laughed it off. She really led a very ordinary life and had nothing interesting to hide.

Suddenly she heard a voice. "What's your name?" Sarah jumped out of her chair, dropping her wine glass on the balcony floor. The glass shattered, scaring her even more. "Who's there?!", she shouted, peering into her lounge room, but she could see no-one.

"It's ok, it's us, the cats", and then she saw the two cats looking at her from within her vision of them.

"What, you speak English?!" Sarah still wasn't believing what she was hearing.

"Just a little," the other cat spoke with a sweet gentle voice. Sarah then realised they were male and female, the female being slightly larger than the male, otherwise they were identical.

"Wow, that's fantastic! And all this time we could have been talking?"

"No, not really, we had to wait until your brain got used to the impulses we send you, but you've done well, now it's second nature to you, just like it is for us, we're born able to do it of course."

"Whoa, that is amazing!" Sarah was now walking around her apartment, she just couldn't keep still. "Do you speak to each other in English, I mean between the two of you?"

"It's not actually speaking, what was your name? We think, and the other person hears, if you can understand that. We don't actually speak aloud, we prefer not to, it's rather loud when you hear the sound as well, like you're doing now".

"Oh sorry, so you can hear me now?" and mid-sentence Sarah stopped speaking aloud and just thought the thought.

"Yes we understand your thoughts."

"Gee, I wonder if we need language at all?" Sarah thought that was a pretty clever question and she was proud of herself.

"I don't know," the male cat was obviously getting bored, and walked away from the other one, out of sight.

"My name is Sarah, and what is yours? You're a female?"

"Yes, Serena, and he is Dargon, pleased to meet you."

"Can you talk to all humans?" Dargon then returned to the conversation and
answered, "No, very few have 'the gift' as you humans call it."

"Oh, so who are they and where are they?"

"There are certain individuals in every race but we can't hear all of them, it's just luck really, if we come across one."

"And I'm one of them! I can hear you, this is great, I can talk to animals! Hey wait a minute, I can't talk to the animals at work, what's the deal, you're sort of different aren't you?"

"We are bred from an ancient telepathic breed of felines' originating from the planet Quatar, six solar systems away from earth. We are a declining species as we mate for life and our breeding cycle comes only once in our lifetime. Also when one of a pair dies, the other dies also. When I get sick Serena gets sick, so we take very good care of each other."

"I'm sorry, it sounds a bit precarious really, and I don't know if you've noticed but I've started feeling what you feel".

"Yes, actually Sarah, you are a particularly sensitive

telepathic. That is not necessarily a good thing. You must now learn to block sometimes, do you know what I mean?"
"Yes but I tried to block you and couldn't".
"We will help you but you must learn, it is a very dangerous thing to feel another's senses and you must learn to control it".
"Ok thanks, but why would you care about what I do?"
"You have become very special to us Sarah, and we would like to help you with your gift. It is very special and very rare. We know that you care for animals, as some people do not. And now you must learn to use your gift in the right way."
"Thank you both. You're very special to me too".

THE MEETING OF THE MINDS, OR NOT

Sarah felt a strong pain in her head and she fell to her knees. Her eyes were shut but she could see a large man in front of her wielding something in his right hand. He flung his arm first back and then forward, and Sarah felt a sharp searing pain in her left thigh. She realised then that the large man held a whip, a long one, similiar to one that she'd seen riders use on horses on the Rodeo planet. The two terrified cats cowered in the corner of a concrete enclosure, but it was small, and there was no escape. The man was relentless in his intent and the lashings he bestowed on the two helpless animals continued for minutes, and then he was gone, back through the door he had come from. Then from the same door came their regular handler, and tended their wounds with a healing spray. The cats could tell he was distressed by what had happened to them but they also understood that he too, was governed by the large man with lots of trinkets. He coaxed them back into their travelling cage and they were again returned to their present living area and left alone. Sarah felt the increasing despair in the cats demeanour as they curled up close together to comfort each other and recover. Then her vision of them faltered and closed. She instinctively put her hand on her left leg but the pain had disappeared.

"Sarah!" She heard her name and remembered she was in her office. "Yes, sir?", she looked up to see her boss, David Spencer of the Earth Intelligence Agency, EIA, scowling at her above her desk.
She still couldn't believe she was working for the

governments intelligence agency. The most secretive society on the planet, no one even knew if they really existed. But she did know now of course, and was so surprised when they approached her, and she thought it was a joke at first. But apparently she was the ideal candidate, an unimportant person in an irrelevant job with no family ties. It would have been insulting if it wasn't so exciting. She jumped at the opportunity of course, and found herself doing loads of computer filing for months. She didn't know that she had actually been chosen for her specific animal skills by the agency, and they had to trial her for a certain amount of time before they decided if she was suitable for the role. She was almost deciding that cleaning up after animals was more exciting than this would ever be when suddenly she was given her first assignment.

"Ah, sorry sir, just dropped my-ah pen sir," she said, picking herself up from the floor.
"I have an assignment for you Sarah, but first you must do some training, you up for it?"
"Oh yes, of course sir, finally".
"Pardon?"
"Oh, nothing sir, yes absolutely, sir!"
"Good, this is my best man, Karl Harper, and he'll be supervising your training. Karl, this is Sarah Whitnish, animal trainer."
"Oh hello," stuttered Sarah as she shook the hand that Karl had reached toward her.
" Uh, I don't actually train the animals, just take care of their feeding, clean their housing, their droppings, etc., exciting stuff like that, you know", she looked away, realising she was blabbering nervously at the sight of this gorgeous looking man standing in front of her. Karl was tall, with short cropped blond hair, as if the sun was always shining on it, and he had

obviously been working out as his arms were bulging out of his skimpy tee, as if it could hardly hold him in. She wondered if he dressed like that deliberately but realised she was letting her mind wander. All of a sudden Sarah found herself lost for words.

"Nice to meet you, and welcome to the team", Karl said.

"Thanks, you too, I mean nice to meet you too, um", Sarah was feeling suddenly young and foolish, even though she thought he couldn't be that much older than she was.

"Ok then, tomorrow at 6.00am sharp in the shed", David Spencer said and walked out the door, leaving her alone with Karl.

But Karl didn't seem to notice that she was feeling uncomfortable. "So you know where to go in the morning, did they give you the 'tour'?" he asked, staring straight at her.

"Oh ah, yes, of course, ah yes they did, thank you." she stammered, looking anywhere in the room but at him.

"Ok, see you then, bright and sparky!" And he was gone too. Bright and sparky? At 6.00 am? Sarah really wished she was more of a morning person.

"You are 8.6 minutes late precisely, young lady", Karl said, tapping his watch.

'You're kidding me right?' Sarah thought, but she said "Yeah sorry, buses,
you know", she tried to sound convincing.

"Right, on with it, we start with the military fitness course and then we'll move on to more strategic sort of training, ok?"

"Oh, sounds great", she hoped she sounded more motivated than she felt.

After what seemed like hours of jumping over things, crawling under things, and climbing up and down other things, Sarah was exhausted and Karl finally called it quits.

"We'll have the results of your fitness test in the morning and then we may have to schedule in some regular training, how do you feel about that Miss. Whitnish?"

"Ah, call me Sarah, and I suppose so".

"We really need you to be in peak physical shape Sarah, and unfortunately it takes a lot of work to get there".

"Ok, no problem", she didn't know whether he was being sarcastic or not.

"Ok break 1 hour for lunch and I'll see you back for theory work, you may find that a bit easier", and with that he was off. 'Again with the sarcasm?' Sarah wasn't sure but anything would be easier than what she'd just been through.

The theory work did turn out to be much easier, being mainly studying the various geographies of known planets, their populations and their resources for export. Early in the afternoon Karl gave her some assignments and told her not to come back to work until she'd memorised everything, and then he politely left.

Then he suddenly stuck his head back through the door. "And look, no offence but you need to get some regular exercise happening, ok? You need to be fit and ready for anything if you're gonna make it in this place." And he was gone.

And as gorgeous as Karl was, she thought, he was a nerd. And a rude nerd at that. She wasn't that unfit was she? She supposed she'd better do what he said but she felt insulted. She'd show him, she'd come back a goddess! Or as close to one that she could manage anyway.

But what a disappointment, she thought. If nothing else, her bad luck with men was staying constant.

ROYALTY TROUBLE BOUND

Prince Adabi leaned back on the soft cushions and looked up at the huge ceiling, painted with a motif of the goddess Nekhbet, her outstretched wings encircling the inscriptions of the lineage of his royal family. The fancy and intricate etchings continued as far as his eyes could see and beyond, continuing along the roof of the elaborate building.
"Hey look at Odjit, she likes you!", Kahotep elbowed him in the side, laughing.
"That hurt, leave me alone!"

Prince Adabi and Kahotep were virtually inseparable. Their mothers were sisters so they grew up together in the royal palace. Not only were they cousins but they were best friends as well, and did everything together. They were never far away from each other and if one was in trouble the other was somehow involved.
But recently and subtly their lives had started going in different directions. After Prince Adabis' eighteenth birthday his royal duties had measurably increased, and the leisure time he had to spend with his cousins and friends was becoming less and less. He was required to visit the different provinces with his father, meeting with the general population, and coupled with the demands of running the mining operations, which his father was slowly turning over to him, left little chance to do the things he used to. But on the rare occasion that Kahotep insisted they go out together, Prince Adabi found himself not enjoying the gatherings in the same way. He would now become annoyed at Kahos' childish

pranks and his endless stream of young girls
hoping for a royal match.

"Look at her, dabby, she wants youuuu," Kaho said blowing
the alluring girl a kiss, as she swirled around the floor in front
of them.

Odjit was one of the dancing girls who lived in the palace and
they were the highlight of any festival, their bright colourful
costumes and exciting dances mesmerising everyone in the
audience watching. But to Adabi the festivals seemed to be
increasing in number, the population finding any excuse to
celebrate, or to honour the latest god, and tonight was no
exception. It was the festival of the bounty god Geb, and the
people were celebrating the harvests of the season, fruits like
citrus and berries, their
main staples. Actually Zenar did not have changing seasons, it
was warm all the time, but the festivals went on regardless, as
they had done throughout their generations.

There were dancers, musicians, and drummers; and an
abundance of food to satisfy multitudes of attendees.

The royal family were required to be present at all these
festivals and at times direct the ceremonies that were
associated with each one but usually after the formalities were
over, Prince Adabi would quietly retire. His father noticed his
absences and was concerned. But when his father asked him
if anything was wrong he just shrugged it off, and told him he
was just tired, and not to worry. The truth was that Prince
Adabi did not know himself why he wasn't enjoying the
partying the way he used to, he was just restless and at times
dismayed at the extravagant way the people spent their time
and lived their lives. He knew it wasn't their fault, planet Zenar
was a wealthy planet, but he also knew that there were
civilisations less fortunate than theirs. When he had tried to
bring the topic up with his father it had caused an argument
and his father had become angry.

"You cannot possibly understand what our people went through only a generation ago!" he had exclaimed. "You were not born yet so this is all you've known. But Zenar was not always like this. We opened up our hearts and our gifts to other beings and what happened? You know the history, you studied it like every other child born to us must study it. But I remember son, I *do* remember the pain on the faces of all the adults around me as I grew up, relatives who did not return from the surface when we were locked up and us children never being allowed to see the light of day on our own beautiful planet. Do you want that to happen again?! Do you? As the future king of this planet it is your duty to protect us, your people and don't you ever forget it. We will not open our generous hearts to strangers again and I will not hear of this subject again, understand boy?"

"Yes, father, sorry, father"

He'd heard it all before, over and over again. But the thought that they were being ignorant and perhaps even selfish,still troubled him at times and the frequent frivolous celebrations exasperated his feelings. So even though he couldn't identify why he didn't enjoy them anymore he began to withdraw from the festivities and seek out other company and other ways to spend his time. His father and even his cousin, did not know that he spent a lot of time with the religious priests at the temple and even stayed

their for days at a time, silently learning to meditate and fast as they did.

Odjit was a stunning beauty with shiny olive skin and black flowing hair that turned at the edges around her perfectly oval face. Her enormous dark brown eyes sparkled with delight and she had just recently learnt how the boys had started swooning when she appeared near them.

But it was only Adabi she had ever had eyes for; but both her cousins, Adabi and Kahotep, still treated her like the little girl they'd grown up with. She never missed an opportunity to dance up close and right in front of her favourite relative but it was as if Adabi could not see how much she longed for him to look at her. She would practice her dancing with the other girls for hours in the enormous dancing halls in front of the gilded mirrors that ran from floor to ceiling, and during the performances she knew she danced exquisitely, for everyone told her so, but when she looked Adabis' way he would have already left before the performance had ended and she would be shattered.

This time she was determined to get his attention and so she jumped up onto the royal platform and danced on the table in front of him. The older members of the royal household had already retired or she would not have dared doing such an outrageous thing but the parties became quite relaxed and unruly as the hours wore on. She moved enticingly in front of him and grabbed his hands pulling him off the cushions.
"Dance with me Adabi!" she cried.
"No, no, I cant." He pulled his hands away and started walking towards the large exit doors.
Kahotep ran after him. "Where are you going?"
"I'm tired, just to bed." Adabi seemed annoyed.
"It's still early, lets go for a night cap with the dancing girls!"
"No, I don't feel like it, I'll see you tomorrow."
"She loves you, you know."
"Who?"
"Odjit of course, don't tell me you haven't noticed the way she looks at you, you must be blind man!"
"Don't be ridiculous, she's just a kid."
"Haven't you seen the way the other boys look at her now? She's not a kid anymore."
Adabi seemed distracted. "Anyway, you're wrong, I'll see you tomorrow. He repeated himself and left.
"I'll party double on your behalf!" Kahotep called after him, but

he'd already disappeared into the crowd of dancers.
"Where is he?" Odjit bumped into Kahotep in her haste.
"He's left, forget about him." Kahotep tried to move his arms
around her waste.
"Get off me!", then her demeanour changed. "He's gone?" She
punched him hard on the arm and moved away.
"That hurt!" But Kahotep wasn't alone for long as two other
dancing girls began swirling him around in time to the loud
music.

Adabi's personal aid woke him from a troubled sleep. "Good
morning Prince Adabi. Your father has requested an audience
with you this morning. It is now late, he will be waiting Your
Highness."
"Thank you I will get dressed."
Adabi walked down the ornamented corridor that separated
his quarters from his parents. He entered a large circular room
that his father always used to discuss important matters with
the members of the royal family and this morning everyone
was in attendance.
Kahotep and Odjit ran over to him.
"Where have you been sleepyhead?" Kaho nudged him in the
ribs.
"What's this about?"
"We don't know but there are rumours that something bad has
happened." Odjit slid her arm through his and guided him past
the others to the front of the assembly.
His father appeared at the front of the gathering.
"Everybody listen. An event has transpired and as yet we do
not know the seriousness of the situation. Two of our senior
scientists from the Krystal laboratories have disappeared. We
are doing what we can to find out what has happened to them
but as yet we know nothing. I have called this meeting to
inform you of the developments and we are to keep this

confidential at the moment. There is no need for speculation or to alert the public at this stage. Myself and Adabi will be holding meetings with our security teams this morning and we will have a report again at the end of the day. That is all. Thank you for attending. Prince Adabi please meet me in the security building immediately. Everyone else please go on with your regular activities as if nothing unusual has happened. Good day." He then left through the door he had entered from. "What does it mean Adabi?" Odjit held his arm tightly till he pulled it away.
"I don't know, it is unusual though. I better go, see you later." And he nodded to both of them as he left.

"Good, you're here. We have a meeting with the security chief Richter, straight away." They entered the building and walked towards the main office.
"I know who he is father. I talk with him all the time. You must let me handle things a bit more."
"All in good time son. Don't repeat this but we believe this is a major security risk. A space car was registered as entering and departing the same day the two men went missing. We have no reason to believe they would leave willingly."
"They have been kidnapped then?"
"Yes we believe that is the case."
They now came towards some double doors which slid open as they drew nearer. The security chief met them and their brisk strides matched as they moved into the main offices.
  Richter was a tall man who towered above everyone else. His uniform had to be specially made for him as the largest sizes simply did not fit him. Not only was he tall but he was a thick bulk of a man and it was a brave individual who would ever dare to cross him. Of course there was no such person

on the planet. He was a no nonsense individual who took his job very seriously, and rightly so. Krystal Gold was a rare and expensive mineral much in demand by all races and his position was a difficult one. He regularly needed to review the latest advances in security on other planets to make sure they could not infiltrate the measures used on Zenar to regulate all traffic entering or departing the planet, and to oversee personally all exports of Krystal. He was one of the few Zenarians, including his staff, who regularly left the planet in the course of his work.

The three men entered Richters office and the heavy doors closed together behind them.

"I have some news Your Highness, Prince Adabi". He nodded to both of them. "We have traced the ship that left here to a small uninhabited moon two systems away. I will leave today and find out what has become of our two team members."

"No, we need you here. We must review our security and work out what went wrong, and the best person, the only person who can do that is you. Adabi will go and take a security team with him."

"But it is dangerous sire, we have no information on who is on that planet. It is a dangerous security risk for Prince Adabi to leave the planet. We do not know what has befallen our two scientists and we cannot place Adabi in danger."

"Adabi must get to know the outside world now Richter. If not now when? He is a grown man and as responsible for the security of this planet as you are. I'm sorry but the decision is final. We need you here and the only other person who can really be trusted now and who can take responsibility is Adabi. Are you up for it son?"

"Yes father. I will prepare my team immediately."

THE REVELATION

It took Sarah a week before she thought she knew enough about the assignments Karl had given her to go back to work. She knew nerdy-boy would berate her over anything unlearned, so she made sure she knew the details thoroughly. Most of the planets exported normal necessities like food, clothing, arts, jewellery or dealt with manufacturing goods required in the home or business. But there were a couple of planets that stood out, the ones that held resources that had become scarce over time such as water or diamonds. And then there were a very special few spread across the galaxies that held and claimed ownership to essential fuel. One of these was the planet Zenar in Earth's' solar system, that had the only known source of Krystal Gold in the system. Krystal Gold was the substance used to power all types of machinery from the microwave in the kitchen to the power required for transport between planets and systems. Manufactured into the tiniest chip, it could be used to power anything at the speed of light, including travel in real time over extraordinary distances. Security on this planet was extensive with entry completely prohibited except with a permit personally approved by the ruling monarchy. And though they were perceived to be a gentle, albeit reclusive people, they were once under attack by an ancient clan of giants of whom they eventually obliterated completely from their planet. Migration to the planet was entirely restricted except in rare cases of approved marriages. The story repeated itself on planets with similar valuable assets, such as the diamond planet named Ricar, run by a race of people comprised totally of females only; and the currency planets of each solar system which employed individuals from every government race. These planets particularly had substantial security systems either privately or publicly run.

Sarah waited nervously outside David Spencer's office. The secretary had let him know she was waiting but forty minutes had gone by and she was feeling decidedly insignificant. "Sorry to have kept you Sarah, this is agent Tamara, you know Karl and this is agent Dominic Bellarto", David Spencer muttered quickly as he ushered her into his office. "Meet Sarah Witnish, everyone."

Sarah could see that Tamara was not from the human race but from the exotic planet of Tiruni, where all the women had olive skin and luscious long black, perfectly straight hair. Tamaras' was pulled up tightly on her head in a circular bun and her long curved black fingernails prodded it now and then. Her cat-like slanted eyes scrutinised Sarah and made her feel uncomfortable. The Tiruni were a rapacious, arrogant, but highly cultivated civilisation, said to be merciless in combat. They were unusually, asexual, in that they were born with no male or female organs, they were all a single gender. They then took on whatever form they preferred, female, male or neutral. Dominic Bellarto on the other hand was of a typical European background, with curly black hair and a playboy demeanour. They were an odd couple and Sarah wondered how they got on together.

"So nice to meet you," he said, as he lifted her hand and kissed it on the inside palm.

Sarah withdrew it in shock and stammered "Yes, you too."

"Hello," Sarah said to Tamara, but the woman just grunted and turned away.

"Now Sarah you've been through all our security training and you've done some training with Karl and performed in all of them excellently." David spoke while reading something on his desk so she could hardly tell if he was specifically talking to her. He seemed to be talking to no one in particular, but she felt compelled to answer.

"Ah, thank-----" But David cut her off and continued as if he hadn't heard her. " Now we have a mission for you and we're confident you can complete it alone. Karl will give you the details." And with that everyone walked out of the office, Karl grabbing her by the arm and pulling her out also.

"Allow me," Dominic took Sarah's' other arm and guided her down the hall. "Our director can be a bit curt sometimes, my dear. Let me take you for a cup of coffee, may I?" His accent was thick and beguiling.

"I think Miss. Witnish has some work to do." Karl gave her a patronising look.

"Perhaps another time then," and she smiled at Dominic. She looked around but Tamara had disappeared.

"Come into my office and we'll go over the details," Karl said walking off at a brisk pace.

"Au revoir, my lovely." And Dominic swaggered off.

   She followed Karl into his office. He tossed some papers at her and
began talking before she could close the door. "Read those, if you have any questions let me know, your craft is ready, you leave immediately."

   Sarah took a few minutes to read the instructions. She was to travel into the Sahara desert to discover if there were any illegal mining operations being conducted after EI had detected some activity in that area.

"Any questions?" Karl seemed eager to end the session.

"I guess not. It seems pretty straightforward."

"Great, report to me on your return. And remember, all

assignments are hundred percent confidential." He held open the door without looking at her.

"Gee, that man annoys me," she thought. "Does he have to be so unfriendly and condescending?"

Sarah walked to the hovercraft hangar and stepped into the one that had been prepared for her.

On her return from the desert, Sarah went to her office and documented everything she'd seen in detail, as she'd been taught to do in training. When she was happy with the way it was written and had included all of the photos she'd taken, she made an appointment with Karl's assistant to present it to him.

"How did it go?" There were no niceties where Karl was concerned.

"Good, I think." And she placed the report on his desk in front of him.

"Thanks, there'll be a meeting later today. We'll let you know the exact time," he said, without looking up.

Sarah thought some garlic prawns would be a tasty celebratory lunch for her first mission as she walked out of his office.

Sarah could hear arguing as she waited outside David Spencer's' office. She'd been told the meeting would be at 5.00pm and she was early. She recognized Karl s' voice and had never heard him raise his voice or seen him lose his temper, so she was surprised. The secretary acted as though she could not hear a thing and continued doing her work. The voices subsided and the door opened.

"Come in Sarah," David said with a smile. He shut the door behind her.

"Karl thinks you're too young to be part of our little group, how do you feel
about your new job with us?"
Sarah was put on the spot and didn't know what to say. She knew that Karl didn't approve of her and it made her feel inadequate.
"I'm enjoying it immensely so far, sir."
"Well Sarah, I think you're doing brilliantly and you're perfect for what we need right now. And you're report was excellent, I hear." He seemed a different person than the last time she was in his office when he was so abrupt.
"Well it seems there's some illegal activity going on in our Eastern desert area and we need to move on it to close it down. But first we need to find out all we can about who's behind it and what they think they've found. You and Karl will be working on this together. And I know that Karl will be greatly appreciative of your help, wont you Karl." It obviously wasn't a question. "Dismissed."
And Karl walked out.

Sarah stormed into his office. "What is your problem?!"
"You have no experience whatsoever, you're not qualified for this type of work." He said calmly, as if there could be no argument.
"Well I'll bet you weren't either when you first started!" Sarah's' eyes glared.
"For your information I served fifteen years as an Lieutenant in the Marines before I started here and I'd certainly had more life experience by then. I've lived on many different worlds."
"Well David seems more than happy with me so I guess we'll have to get along. Now what do we have to do to find out about this project?"
"Hmm." Karl grunted. "We've traced the materials back to a

guy named Bosworth. You know him?"
"Yes of course, I've seen him on TV."
"It seems he's been hiring some heavy mining equipment
through a small inconspicuous company out of West Africa."
"How do you know this?"
"We have our sources stationed everywhere. No one does
anything without us knowing about it."
"Did my info help?"
"No, we already knew he was there. David just wanted to
warm you up, make sure you could do something on your
own, that's all."
"Warm me up for what?"
"Whatever he has planned for you, I wouldn't know. Now I
need you to go back there, masquerading as a worker, let me
know as soon as they dig something up. We need to know
what's down there. I'll arrange your cover. In the meantime I'll
find out what Bosworth is doing here on Earth. He never goes
anywhere unless he's up to something. Ok?"
"Ok."

Sarah had been at the mine site for a week working in the
kitchen. The name for the job she'd been given was Sonia
McKenzie. One night she was sitting with the others when she
heard a commotion. She ran with the others to where they'd
heard shots coming from but when they ran around the corner
of the building they were surprised to see Bosworth himself
standing next to a hover car. In real life he was even larger
than he looked on the television screen.
"Nothing to worry about folks!", he boomed. "Meet your new
foreman, my right hand man, Fragar. Proceed!" And he pulled
himself into the car and left.
"There'll be a meeting first thing in the mornin' in the mess

room. 8 o'clock sharp. Everyone must be there with bags packed." And Fragar walked off .

The workers started asking each other questions, wondering what might be happening tomorrow, but Sarah went off to quietly contact Karl.

"Something's happening tomorrow," she told him. "Bosworth was just here and put his top guy in charge. Everyone has to have there bags packed by the morning."

"They must have struck gold if I can use the pun. We'll get you out of there tonight. Be ready."

The next day at EI headquarters news came through of a large explosion at a mining site in the Arabian desert. Fifty odd people had been killed and there were no survivors. The mine had been closed down. That was Sarah's' first exposure to the perils of her new profession.

The next week EI found out that Bosworth had applied for a permit to mine on the site, even though an investigation was still pending over the explosion that had happened there. Earth council had refused but Bosworth had then put in an appeal to the solar system council stating that he owned the land and could do whatever he wanted on it. EI had to then find out how he had gained ownership without anyone knowing, but apparently the titles were legitimately bought through one of his trading companies. A court battle loomed and it was Earth Intelligences' job to find out what the mine really contained. They believed it was something more valuable than the iron ore that Bosworth claimed was down in the mine. Iron ore was found on nearly all planets so was not a scarce commodity. Therefore EI was suspicious that Bosworth was going to a lot of trouble to obtain a relatively common metal.

EI sent a team of specialist agents into the mine carrying

investigation papers to examine the cause of the explosion that killed so many people. The mine has twenty four hour guards stationed by Bosworth but they could not refuse entry to the investigative team holding warrants of entry issued by the High Court. The lift carried the probe ten kilometres underground and by remote control would take a sample to return to the surface. The probe was made from steel that could withstand temperatures of up to 4000 degrees Celsius. These deep mines were way too hot for people to venture down without expensive air coolers.

But what they found at the bottom of the mine was the biggest surprise El ever could have imagined. The mine contained Krystal Gold, the rarest and most powerful mineral in all worlds.

TO BATTLE

"Get your ships ready, we're going to battle!"
Even Adabi couldn't hide his excitement. Kaho and Odjit had never seen him like this. Adabi was walking past them as he spoke but Kaho grabbed his arm and swung him around.
"What's going on?"
"You heard me. Get your ships ready, you'll be briefed on the way. We're leaving now!"

Planet Zenar had never seen anything like it. A small army of ships assembling itself to leave and potentially go into battle. An army that had seen intensive training but was never expected to be utilised. But before they could go Prince Adabi was to address the nation that stood in bewilderment before him.
He stepped out onto the podium and his image was being telecast across the whole planet.
"My fellow Zenarians. I think you have all heard by now that two of our eminent scientists were yesterday kidnapped and taken to a moon two solar systems away. Myself and members of my security team will now embark on a rescue mission. It is one of uncertainty and unknown danger but I implore all of you to stay calm and trust in the sovereignty of your rulers and leaders and give us your blessings and prayers as we depart on this journey. We act on behalf of all Zenarians past and present and pledge our loyalty to the planet Zenar!" And with this he held up the staff that their ancestors had carried into battle and that was kept in the royal hall with all the other antiquities.
The Zenarian people had never seen it outside of the royal

palace before so it caused a collective roar when Prince Adabi held it up.

   They then watched in awe as ten travel ships took off and disappeared into the golden sunlit sky.

"Good speech cos." Kaho's ship was set on autopilot so he was now free to talk.

"Thanks but I didn't write it."

"So what's the deal boys?" Odjit placed her ship on autopilot too. "How much do we know about this moon and who's on it?"

"We don't. But the ship with our guys on it was tracked to there and our intel says there's been coming and going from that moon but that's it. They can't identify the players. We're to go in, get the guys back and return home, that's it."

"Not much to work with darlin'."

"Hey leave the lovey dovey stuff for home would ya Odjy?"

"Mind your own business Kaho."

"And you two mind your training. No independent heroics got it?"

"Yes, *Your Highness.*"

"You're spoiling our fun, sweety."

"Be ready, there it is. All ships in formation. We're going in!"

   The ships hovered together on entry and then parted, slowly beginning to encircle the moon. Like most moons the surface was desolate, an arid dry landscape with large craters and old crusty lava flows.

"Anyone see anything?"

"No". "Not a thing". "Nothin'."

"It's too quiet, be alert." But it was too late.

BANG. An explosion sounded across the airwaves.

"We're under attack!" That came from one of the pilots on the other side.

"Hold on! We're coming!"

 But by the time the cousins got around to the other side there was chaos. One ship of theirs was on the ground destroyed, smoke pouring out of it into the sky and a battle was going on above it. Two ships from that team were exchanging fire with a swarm of alien ships and the two others were approaching from the other side opposite the cousins.

"Star team! Go up higher and help them from above, we'll take this side!" Adabi shouted out orders and started shooting his laser gun as he darted into the fray. Odjit and Kahotep followed his lead. He estimated there to be only about ten of the opposing ships and he could tell that they were an outdated model and quite unmatched to their invaders in speed, agility and weaponry. Zenar was an affluent planet and so did not find it difficult to keep up with the latest advances in security, indeed they needed to, so as to protect their Krystal. Three of the antiquated ships were shot down immediately with two more to follow; and with five laying on the ground on fire within seconds, the other five suddenly turned and sped away into the distance.

"Well done guys, but they were really no match for us. "Who's gone?"

"It was Jaapi, sir, they got him from behind before we knew they were there." Qeb from the Star team replied.

"Ok boys they know we're here so lets find our guys and get out. Turn on your trackers and follow them." Adabi switched on his motion tracker and steered in the direction the alien ships had taken. The others pulled in behind him. They immediately caught up and watched the ships hover above ground for a second before a large hangar door opened and they filed inside.

Adabi and his squad hovered above the opening and he spoke this time to his machine. "Detect opening code."

Instantly the hangar door again opened and they followed their attackers inside.

They parked their vessels with no opposition and got out quickly. They were in an old steel factory that had obviously been abandoned for a long time. They walked through an old steel door that was hanging off its hinges into a corridor with empty rooms all along it. Finally they came to another door that was closed but the locks were broken. They opened it to a welcoming party.

"Hold up your hands!" But Adabi and his men were too quick and weren't expected to put up a fight. But Zenarians were trained for no mercy and they gave none, especially with one of their own already slain by ambush outside. Five men lay dead on the floor in front of them and Adabi peered closer at their faces. "Goblins. No wonder they can't fight. What are they doing so far from home? Always mixed up in something too big for them to handle." Goblins got their name from the way they looked. A short green skinned people with long curved noses and stocky bodies, they were known and despised as sticky beaks, poking their noses into affairs that were none of their business.

"Ok spread out, see what you can find."

"They're here!" Qeb called from a back room. But the goblins had got to them first. The two scientists lay dead. Both of them shot in the head.

Back on Zenar Adabi had a meeting with his father, the king, and Richter, the security chief.

"What happened son?"

"Goblins, just goblins, and they killed our men before we could get to them." Adabi looked down in shame.

"I'm sorry father, I failed."

"No you did well, nothing could have saved them after they'd seen you. Goblins are a simple and vile people. They probably

panicked and no doubt enjoyed doing the deed."
Richter interrupted. "Did you find anything about who and why they'd been taken? Goblins couldn't have done it by themselves so who was it?"
"No there was nothing at all. No sign of anyone else and apart from a few old factories, the moon was deserted. The ships were old and hardly working, they could have come from any old salvage yard." Adabi was feeling frustrated that he hadn't found out more.
But his father was reassuring. "We've tightened security and we'll keep our eyes open. Well done son, I'm proud of you."
"Yes Adabi, good job". Richter opened the door. "Make sure you look after your team."

The next few months went on as usual and no more threats arose. Security remained high but Adabi's father had decided they were too ignorant of what was going on in the outside world. He thought that Zenar may have become a target because they were so sheltered and insulated and perhaps it was time to change that. If they were ever to find out exactly who had violated their security and killed two of their top specialists, they would now need to re-enter the world stage. They would do it carefully and subversively but they would become experts on world affairs and establish the authority the Zenarian people commanded with the demand for Krystal. And Prince Adabi was the key. He had proven himself able to lead and accomplish a deadly mission and he was now to begin visiting other planets and become more familiar with important proceedings and prominent people.
And so Adabi and his cousins left Zenar more and more and started experiencing other civilisations and how they lived. Adabi began attending solar system council meetings that he had in the past sent a delegate to in his place and would

personally represent Zenar publicly on any occasion requiring it. He travelled with Richter and his men as his personal bodyguards and was becoming well known on the planets' arena.

But it was not all work and Kahotep made sure they enjoyed their campaigns abroad.

QUATAR

"You must try harder, control and block". Dargon was
becoming frustrated.
"I can't, it just won't work for me!" Sarah had been trying for
weeks to block out the cats' thoughts when they asked her to,
but she seemed to have no control over when they came and
when they stopped.

Some days, after Sarah finished work at the animal
sanctuary, she had spent many hours looking up all the
information she could find on the planet Quatar. It was six
galaxies away and as such, would take a prolonged trip of
days at a time to get there if she'd wanted to. Travel would be
on a ship equipped for such a long voyage through space, the
time capsules could only transport you from planet to planet
over a certain distance.

Quatar was, it seemed from all she read, an extremely exotic
planet. It's distance from other galaxies meant that it had been
shielded from civilization for a long time, enabling an animal
hierarchy that had taken centuries to evolve. A lush, rich green
planet covered primarily with vast grasslands that supported
an abundance of herbivores, developed into an ideal
environment for predatory species to flourish and evolve, from
large birds to exotic cats like the ones Sarah knew. Some
animals had developed an intelligence unheard of on other
planets, ripe for exploitation when finally discovered by human
equivalent races. Only a recent discovery, all the animals on
the planet had been plundered and removed into captivity,
spread throughout the known worlds. The grasses on the
planet had then spread unchecked, with no animals to graze
upon them, until a global fire had reduced the planet to an

uninhabitable desert. The fire, visible from distant satellites, had been telecast around the worlds, it was big news on the days it burned. Most of the animals had subsequently died after being exposed to adverse and unfamiliar environments on other worlds, the remaining few who managed to survive were scattered throughout the innumerable galaxies. Councils of governments had made it illegal to own any of these listed missing species on their planets, but they quickly disappeared into private collections, never to be heard of again.

"Dargon, she's trying, give her a rest, please". Serena was more sympathetic, but Sarah thought even she was beginning to grow weary with the slow progress of trying to block the cats thoughts from her mind.
There'd been no progress at all actually, and even Sarah herself had now
had enough.
"Yes, please Dargon, I want to stop now, I'm sorry, I've tried".
"Yes, let's stop", he replied.
"I saw what happened to you and your planet, it's gone isn't it, no good anymore", Sarah's' voice trailed off, she didn't know whether they wanted to be reminded of the devastation they had endured.
"You've seen?!", Serena's' ears instantly pricked up, her eyes intense.
"Well, I just saw what was on the news that's all", Sarah suddenly realizing they may not know about the total destruction of their planet.
Dargon was also now looking at her intently, and she was momentarily uncomfortable under their gazes.
"Well how much do you know?" She thought she'd play it safe, she did not want to distress them further, especially as it seemed they were one of the few who had survived and were doing well.

She wished now that she hadn't brought it up at all.

"We can tell you what happened to us, that's all we know."
Serena's' face suddenly darkened, a sad despairing look
came into her eyes and her head hung low as she recounted
the shocking details of the events that unfolded on her home
planet.

"First we saw objects in the sky that we'd never seen before.
They would fly around in the sky for weeks, and then one day
strange life forms came down and walked around, here and
there, looking at us, and at all the other animals, trying to talk
to us but none had the gift. Then over several months, more
and more ships came, and more and more different types of
people, and they took the animals. There was nowhere to
hide, the people seemed to be everywhere at once, and they
could move from one place to another in seconds, and of
course we could only run, but it did no good. They would shine
a beam of light on us, and then we could not move anymore.
We were then taken up into their ship like all the others had
been, and we've never heard anything since. Now please,
Sarah, tell us what has become of our home?!"

Sarah knew she could not tell them the truth of what was left
of their planet, the desperate look in their eyes left her in no
doubt of that. But what could she say? She didn't want to give
them an outright lie, but she also did not want to dash their
hopes altogether.

"Well the news did not say much about the planet itself, it just
said that most of the animals had been captured and
disappeared."

"Oh is that all?" Serena seemed more than disappointed. "We
know that already".

"Was there something in particular you wanted to know
Serena?" Sarah had gotten the impression there was
something Serena wasn't telling her, something else she
wanted information about.

"Nothing, no nothing". Dargon said gruffly.

Sarah wanted to dig deeper but Dargon turned, signalling the meeting was over, and Sarah was relieved they hadn't wanted to know any more details.

The connection between the animals and herself closed abruptly, and Sarah lay in bed, troubled, and not able to sleep.

THE SEA PLANET

The three cousins were standing at the bar of the party planet Squash, perfectly situated for social gatherings right in the middle of the solar system. They were laughing and joking, sampling the different cocktails on offer. Richter and his men were a few tables away, doing the same. It had become a familiar scenario for the Zenarians when they were away from home and they were beginning to get a reputation as larrikans around the social scene of solar system 8. And because Richters' reputation preceded him, it was a brave or ignorant man who messed with them.

Adabi was the quiet one who tended to stay back and watch Kahotep make a fool of himself fighting and drinking, and Odjit was the risk taker going places she perhaps should not have been going; but Adabi was always there to rescue them or back them up from their latest folly.

This night as usual Adabi was deep in thought, as he and his father were contemplating raising the price of Krystal to reflect the state of the marketplace. All resources and elements were becoming more rare as time went on and the prices had to reflect that fact.

"Hey Cos, time to stop working and start playing!" Kahotep was always on the lookout for the next good time. "Listen I heard about this crazy planet in SS4 that's all water. Just think of that. The whole planet is an ocean run by 'Mer' people, people that live in the sea, and sea creatures ferry you around. It's just one great big resort. Wanna try it?"

"Sure why not."

"Ok let's go. Hey Richter, we're off to the sea planet. I'll send your ship the coordinates." Kahotep walked over to where a

large bear-man had been leaning all over Odjit and whispering in her ear. "We're going Odjy. Comin?"
"She'll come when she's ready to come." The bear man said glaring at Kaho and not taking his arm from around her shoulders.
"She's coming now, isn't that right Odjy?" Kaho's voice had now become insistent.
The bear man then got up from his seat and stood between Kaho and Odjit. "And who says so?!" he boomed.
Kaho took a step forward and pushed against the man even though his head only reached up to the man's chest.
"I do, that's who."
Richter then saw what was happening and stood up but Odjit moved between the two men and put her back to Kaho.
"It's ok Hora, it was good meeting you but I have to go. See you again sometime."
The bear-man grunted and sat back down. Then they all followed Odjit out.

   The sea planet was a brilliant blue from the window of the space ship. Entry to this planet was by a holiday booking only and Odjit had taken care of that on the way. As their two ships came into orbit they were locked on to the planets control system and guided in to a smooth landing onto the water.
   They stepped out onto the landing platform and were amazed to see a world of blue. Blue sky met blue sea, and buildings made from blue tinted glass sprung out of the water as far as they could see. They were met by a welcoming party of Mer people, people that not only had two legs to walk on but they had a tailfin for swimming dragging behind them. Their skin was covered in scales as was their tail, and their hands and feet were webbed. Both men and women had long flowing hair which was tied up behind their backs.
"Welcome to our planet. As it is your first time here we would

request you attend a short presentation to familiarize yourselves with our facilities. We are sure you will enjoy your visit. Please come this way."

They followed their hosts into the glass building and to the presentation room.

"Please sit down. The video has a duration of five minutes." As soon as they took their seats, refreshments came up through the floor and stopped next to each of their armrests. The plates were filled with morsels of seafood with glasses of champagne and water beside them.

With the video over they retired to their rooms, agreeing to meet in an hour in the lobby of the hotel situated on the ocean floor. Each room was below sea level, with its own view of the sea around it. From the comfort of their hotel room they could watch the ocean life going on outside the wall to ceiling windows; the sharks, stingrays and all types of fish swimming past them, unaware they were being watched by the thousands of tourists that visited every week.

From the video they had learned that the Mer people were caretakers of the planet not only for themselves but also for the marine population. They spoke the same language as the more intelligent marine life such as the dolphins and whales and larger sea creatures, and farmed the smaller fish populations to ensure an ongoing supply of seafood for all beings on the planet.

All planets on arrival, took a record of a visitors name and originating planet and charged a fee to that home planet that covered the activities that they engaged in. That was the common practice in all solar systems.

But the Mer people monitored their whole eco system of the sea they lived in so successfully, that they had no need for any outside assistance and therefore did not charge any fees at all for the tourists to holiday on their planet. It was truly a unique experience and therefore drew interest from diverse cultures all over the galaxies.

The cousins met in the vast lounging area on the floor level of the hotel and walked around the windows amazed at the many different types of sea creatures swimming past them.
"Hey Adabi, I've got a riddle for you. Which one of us is in the aquarium, them or us?!"
"I guess it's us. Good one, Kaho."
"Hey boys, did you know you can go swimming in there with them? They put you in an air bubble and you just swim around with the fishes." Odjit looked resplendent in a deep green gown that set off her dark olive skin and her mischievous brown eyes. "Are you boys game or you scared of the sharks?"
"I *am* scared of the sharks! I don't fancy becoming fish stew myself Odjy." Kaho
looked as one glided past close to the window, one of its eyes seemingly fixed on him as it swam away.
"Actually they can't penetrate the bubble material, whatever it's made of. Otherwise they'd have dead tourists all over the place. Scaredy cat." She pinched Kaho's arm as was her habit of doing.
"We'll go tomorrow morning then. Sounds like fun." Adabi couldn't take his eyes off the windows either, like everyone else.
"Fun? You wouldn't know fun if it bit you in the butt Cos! Now that there could be fun, whaddya think princey?" Kaho nudged Adabi in the direction of two giggling women walking past, obviously from the planet Canovis with their short cropped purple locks and pale purple skin.
"They've got weird bumps all over their body Kaho, how could you find them attractive?" Odjit looked disgusted.
"Well you probably look horrible to them. It takes all types you know. At least I don't go for bear women. Now that's going too far."

"Speaking of bear men, there he is. Funny coincidence." Adabi nodded to the far end of the room where Hora, the guy from the bar on Turin was standing with some friends. "You'll take all types, you mean Kaho!" And he started walking in the direction of the food hall. "Let's get something to eat, I'm starving."

A few days had gone by and Adabi had begun to feel a bit queezy from eating seafood every day. He was getting restless, even though their days had been filled with activities like boating, water skiing and diving.

Kaho didn't want to admit it but he was tiring of the holiday as well. They were arguing about which day to go home at one of the many bars spread throughout the complex when Hora walked in with some of his bear mates.

"Hi Odjit, we meet again." And he swung his huge arm across her shoulders. But she had since tired of his assuming familiarity and swung it off again.

"What are you doing here Hora?" She looked away, sipping her drink, not really caring if she got an answer or not.

"Holidaying, just like you I guess. Wanna dance?"

"Ah no thanks, not right now."

"Well how about getting cozy in a corner then huh?"

Odjit stood up, she was not one to be picked up so easily and she was beginning to get annoyed with his advances.

"Look it was ok talking to you the other day but now I think you need to leave me alone, right?" She stood squarely in front of the big man and he stepped back in surprise, even though she was only half his height.

That was when his friends started laughing and he decided to take offence. "You bloody Zenarians, think you're royalty or somethin."

It was then that Kaho couldn't help himself. "We are royalty mate!" And he stepped in and shoved the bears stomach with his two hands. But Hora was too heavy and though he went back a couple of steps, quickly composed himself and pushed Kaho right back. Then it was on and Kaho threw the first punch squarely in the middle of the bears belly. One of his mates was about to join in but Adabi stepped in front of him and it was something about the authority in which Adabi looked at him that made him step back and change his mind.

It wasn't long until the Mer police came and threw both Hora and Kaho into separate holding cells. The fight on the Sea Planet was all over the news and it was Richter who told Adabi they had been ordered home by the King. Apparently Adabi had an invitation from a new client wanting to purchase a large quantity of Krystal.

Kaho was turned over to be the responsibility of Richter and they left for the journey home. They don't know what happened to Hora or how long he had to stay in the jail cell on the planet.

But they did know that the King and Queen would not be happy.

THE PRINCE AND THE WHITE CITY

The city was an extraordinary white. Prince Adabi of Zenar had just arrived on planet Bosworth to do some business with the tycoon Bosworth himself. He was not surprised that the well known businessman was wanting to trade in crystal, everyone did, it was a rare commodity in short supply, in fact the only known source in solar system 8 was on his own planet, Zenar; but he was slightly apprehensive when Bosworth requested him to be a personal guest on his planet. Usually Adabi tended to err on the reserved side, but lately his ailing father was encouraging him to be more amicable and outgoing. He was the only heir, his father had said, and as such must become adept at dealing with all kinds of races and any situations that may present themselves. He must, his father insisted, see more of the outside world. The fact was that Bosworth was notorious for never letting anyone at all visit his planet. And therefore Adabi's father maintained that it was a great honour that he had been the very first to receive such an invitation himself.

So against the princes' usual habit of politely refusing any invitation, his father had urged him to accept this one, a request from a widely recognized figure, it could only be good for business, and so he'd accepted.

On arrival, Prince Adabi was ushered into a single aircar, separated from his bodyguards. Before they could object the lone driver flew off leaving his entourage to be placed into other cars that were waiting. This was an unusual practice that just never happened, but he thought instead of being unduly alarmed at the separation of himself and his guards, he would heed his fathers' words and contend with it. Planet Bosworth was a relic of a planet, one of the many that were destroyed in the great war of the past millenium, and left abandoned to float around the galaxy until someone bought it from the solar system committee responsible, in this case solar system 8; the earth's' solar system. The planet was an industrial wasteland, covered in factories, and only Bosworth himself knew what he was developing on it. Prince Adabi's' minders investigated as much as they could about every potential customer, but it turned out that the details of Bosworths background was very sketchy, and hardly any information could be sought. Apparently he was from a distant solar system and the origin of his wealth was somewhat obscure, but that was all they could find out. But as his name was constantly in the news for his latest extravagant acquisition, he seemed simply to be an outlandish newcomer to the local business community.

In the distance Prince Adabi could see a bright light up ahead, but as the car moved closer, he realized it was a huge, giant white bubble, an artificial atmosphere, that they were about to fly over. He asked the driver to slow down as he could not believe what he was seeing. Below the hovering car was a city, a pure white city encased completely in a huge clear white bubble.

"What is that?" the prince asked.

But the driver did not answer.

"Please, stop for a minute," he pleaded, but he could not take his eyes off the scene in front of him.

"Ah, what the hell", said the driver, and set the aircar down beside the bubble city.

Prince Adabi got out and put his face against the clear enclosing material. As he looked on it began to snow inside the city, small white flakes forming a carpet of velvet on the ground. But floating in the air, and walking across the snow, were the most beautiful and delicate white maidens that he had ever seen. As pale as the land they lived in, with white gowns and long white hair trailing behind them, blowing in the light breeze, they rested on the air or tiptoed barefoot on the snow with their pallid white feet. They looked pure and innocent in their secluded world and he thought nothing would be able to disturb the serene beauty of the scene. He looked at the fine, delicate, soft features of their faces and realised they did not know that they were being watched. He longed for one of them to look up and acknowledge him but he wasn't sure why. He felt a strange longing to reach out to them, to talk to them, just to look into the eyes of one of them, and he knew if he did he would fall in love forever.

Just then, as if she had read his thoughts, one of the flawless maidens lifted her head and looked right into his eyes. He was taken aback, and drew in his breath sharply, but he stared, mesmerised, her pale blue eyes piercing into his soul. And just as quickly she lowered her eyes and turned away again; but not before he caught a glimpse of the extreme sadness that emanated from them.

"Hey, we gotta go", the driver said gruffly.

And as the car moved into the distance, the white city disappeared.

Finally the driver slowed and lowered the car onto a wide roof. This building was obviously different to the stark mercantile exterior of the factories that spread across the planets surface. The external material of this one was ultra modern, the latest technology in building structures, and Prince Adabi was reminded   that he was here on business. The driver directed him to a blue square outlined on the ground and instantly he was being elevated at speed downwards into the building. The doors opened and an imposing figure strode into the small space.

"Welcome! Welcome to my home!", he bellowed, as if he was

shouting to someone afar off.

"Thank you", Adabi stepped back in surprise, but Bosworth swung his bulky arm across his shoulders and ushered him out of the elevator.

"So glad you could make it, friend!", he bellowed again, as they ventured down a luxurious gilt lined hallway. Two doors silently retreated into the walls on either side and opened into a vast circular living area. The walls were lined with the same gold material as the hallway, as were the lounge chairs that ran right around the whole room. In the middle was a sunken lounge, filled with one large cushion to lie on.

"Come, Prince Adabi, I will show you to your room", Bosworth motioned to doors at the other side of the room.

"Where are my guards, Mr. Bosworth, have they arrived?"

"Yes, yes, call me Hugh, yes they're in their rooms as well!"

Everything Bosworth said seemed to be extremely loud to Prince Adabi, and he felt slightly intimidated, so he followed quickly, trying to keep up with the hasty walking pace of his raucous
host.

"Here we are, make yourself comfortable and when you are ready, press the green button and my man will come and get you for some grub, huh?!"

"Some what?"

"Grub, food, dinner man!", and with that Bosworth gave him a shove and the door closed behind him.

Prince Adabi showered and changed, and knew that he should be thinking about the details of the business deal he would be making with Bosworth. But he could not stop thinking about the beautiful snow white girl with the piercing light blue eyes. The picture of her in her world of snow stayed in his mind, and the many questions of who she was, where did she come from and what was she doing on Bosworth's planet played round and round in his mind. Although he knew it was none of his business, and against protocol to never interfere with other peoples' affairs, he decided he would just ask some simple questions about her and find out if he could be given an introduction. Yes, he decided he wanted to, had to meet this beguiling woman that had, in an instant, captured his attention and maybe even his heart.

There was a brief, sharp knock on the door and Prince Adabi followed the driver of his aircar down the hall. Either Bosworth was low on staff or perhaps he preferred this man to take care of his important duties. The large doors that slid open as they approached revealed a long expanse of a room with a lengthy dining table along one side and a lounging area along the other. Behind the length of the dining table along the wall was the image of a flowing river, cascading through a lush green rainforest of ferns and tall beech trees. The opposite wall behind the lounge chairs was a huge screen telecasting the latest news and entertainment.

A door opened from the other side and Bosworth burst through.

"Come! Sit down my fellow!", he announced taking long hurried strides towards them.

"Go, get the meal!", he waved his arm at the driver and thrust his huge hand into the Princes', shaking it violently.

"How's your room Prince?"

"Fine, thank you very much. More than comfortable." Although the prince was used to lavish palaces on his own planet he was ever-polite to his business associates.

"I hope you like sansushi, it's on the menu tonight!" Bosworth strode past the long dining table to a smaller round one at the other end of the room.

"Yes, of course, one of my favourites."

"Sit down." Bosworth motioned to one of the chairs and then

leaned with both hands on the one next to it. "I'm so sorry but I cannot stay, I have an issue that just came up, but please make yourself comfortable and I will see you first thing in the morning. Please help yourself to anything you may need, the kitchen with instant food ordering from any planet is just through there, and Fragar will tend to anything else you request." And before the prince could answer he went back through the door he had come from.

Straight after, Fragar, the driver, came through the kitchen doors with a banquet of delicious morsels based on the freshest of seafood, octopus, salmon and bright red roe.
"My men, are they joining me?", the prince asked.
"They've already eaten", he answered gruffly.
"Well, where are they?"
"They have their own quarters, sir." And with that he exited through the same door Bosworth had.
The prince was aghast at being left alone in the enormous room but realised he had no choice but to accept the situation. The meal was delicious and after watching the world news for a while, decided to have an early night and be alert and ready for the discussions in the morning. He sipped some of the excellent red wine from the bottle Fragar had left on the table, and fell asleep readily on the eloquent bed in his room.

In the morning the prince awoke to the hot sun streaming blindingly through the large windows of the bedchamber. He put his hand to his head and remembered that he'd drank the wine last night. Maybe he'd consumed more than he thought. He looked at the time and realised he'd slept in considerably which was odd because he never slept in. He was like his own personal alarm clock, waking up at the same time every day, which was fortunate as on his planet there was no night and day, no darkness, and no morning to distinguish from the night.

It was now eleven o'clock and he wondered what Bosworth must think of him sleeping so late. He hoped he wasn't inconveniencing him.

He quickly showered, dressed and checked his appearance. He looked like he hadn't slept for a week and again berated himself for drinking too much, although he didn't think he'd had enough to knock him out and give him a hangover. He picked up his laptop and went into the main room but it was empty. He looked around for an intercom to talk to someone but could not find one, and then walked to the door. He tried to push it open but it would not budge. He tried to pull it but it wouldn't move. He walked around the room in bewilderment and then tried to push open the door again. He was sure he'd seen the two men go through it last night. It was the only door in the room.

"Hello? Hello?!", he cried out but it seemed no one could hear. He ordered something to eat and then opened his PC. But he found it could not connect to the outside world. He thought that Bosworth must be busy and berated himself for getting up so late.

The day wore on and the prince busied himself with some work on his computer and keeping himself up to date with the news on the broadcast. When evening came he again tried to open the door that the men had left through but to no avail. He knocked on the door and shouted through it but no one answered. Late at night he became agitated and wondered why his guards did not look for him. Eventually he fell asleep on the gold luxurious couches and the days repeated themselves, day after day, night after night. On the fourth morning Prince Adabi looked dishevelled and had fallen asleep again on the couch in his clothes. He had gone through feelings of confusion, anger, panic and subsequently desperation, and was now in a constant state of mild hysteria. He had not eaten since the second day and would wake constantly in the night not knowing where he was.

Suddenly the door opened and Bosworth and Fragar marched in. They moved between the lounge chairs and stood over him. Prince Adabi jumped up and began straightening his clothes and running his hands over his hair. But Bosworth shoved him back down into the couch and threw a piece of paper and a ballpoint pen at him.

"Sign this Zenar and you can go!" , he said fiercely.

"What?"

"You heard me, sign it! Or you'll stay here till you do! Your men are all dead, you're all alone, my prisoner!" , and he let out a rapacious grunting sound. And again the two men left.

The prince read the printed words and as he did so he experienced all the emotions again, confusion, bewilderment, anger and last of all helplessness. He banged on the doors and the walls with his fists, and he wondered could his trusted companions really be dead? But he knew that Bosworth spoke the truth and wondered how he could have been so foolish to have come to his planet; especially after the events of the past year. He briefly blamed his father and then felt ashamed of the thought, knowing that his father must, at this very moment, be beside himself with guilt and remorse and worry for persuading his only son to travel to an unknown planet.

The prince read the transcript again. 'I, Prince Adabi Zenar, of the planet, Zenar, in my right mind and testament, hereby transfer all deposits and holdings of Gold Krystal to Hugh Bosworth of Planet Bosworth.' The document was dated with today's date and had a space for the prince to write his signature. Unbelievably at the top of the page was Planet Zenar's insignia and emblem, and Prince Zenar then understood the seriousness of his situation. He tried to connect his laptop again with the outside world but knew that it was futile. He wondered why his kidnapping wasn't on the news and then realised that he had been watching the same newsreel over and over again. He was a captive, a prisoner of this mysterious, conniving brute of a man; and that man wanted everything that he owned. His people would become slaves again or even worse, banished from their own planet, and he could not let that happen. Fleetingly, the beautiful white woman with the sad eyes crossed his mind, and he then knew that she must be a prisoner also. This was why Bosworth never let anyone enter his planet and why he was so secretive. And he had made it so easy for him, just entering his planet so trusting and unsuspecting. But Bosworth was a malevolent and ruthless man who would not hesitate to kill him and indubitably planned to do just that. What was it he wanted from the snow princesses he wondered, and how many times had he gotten away with this before? He was obviously a very brazen criminal and therefore must have a well thought out plan. But the one thing he did not know about Prince Adabi was that he came from resolute stock and he could be a formidable adversary.

EARTH TO THE RESCUE

The memo was in everyone's email and a physical copy was on everyone's desk first thing in the morning. Must be important, Sarah thought.

All
agents
to attend meeting in the office of
D. Spencer
at
800 hours

She picked up the memo and looked at it. She was an agent wasn't she? Yes that meant her. She still didn't feel important enough to be included in that little group, but she had no choice but to turn up. Karl interrupted her thoughts.
"Sarah come to my office before the meeting, need your autograph."
"Autograph?"

"You know, just your signature on some papers."
"Oh, ok." And she followed him down the corridor.
"There you go, sign where the x's are and we'll be off. Seems you've passed your probationary period, congratulations."
"Really? Thank you Karl!"
"Don't thank me, it all goes through the system and David makes the final decision. I'll see you in his office when you're done. Just leave them there on my desk. He placed the pen he'd been holding on top of the forms and walked out.
Wow she'd passed her probation. She couldn't believe it. She could tell Karl wasn't pleased but she really didn't care what he thought any more But she would prove herself to him with time, she decided. Now that she was a fully fledged 'spy', she felt a new confidence rising, she could do anything.
Unfortunately she couldn't tell her friends though, it was all confidential; as far as they knew she had a new administration job with the government.

  But she could feel a prawn and white wine dinner coming up tonight! What a shame Karl wouldn't celebrate with her. He was the only one she really spoke to at all in the agency, it really wasn't the thing for agents to mix with the other staff. They all seemed incredibly busy and even she was kept on her toes. And every mission was shrouded in secrecy, she could not breathe a word about them to anyone except her immediate superiors, it was in her contract. She signed the last page with an exaggerated flourish and was about to put down the pen when she noticed an inscription on it. 'To My Son Karl' it read. So the ogre had parents. She realised it must be a treasured item so she kept it in her hand as she went to the meeting, intending to give it to Karl when she got there. But her colleagues were in full discussion already when she walked into her boss' office so she forgot about the pen.

"Sarah, glad you could make it, close the door, take a seat.

David was in serious mode.

"We've been given a job by the security council to attend the planet Zenar. Apparently the heir to the throne Prince Adabi Zenar has gone missing. He's been missing now for nearly a week and his father King Ptah has asked the council for help in locating him. So speed up your knowledge of all things Zenar and I will remind you all that it is the only planet in our solar system that supplies Krystal Gold. I think that speaks for itself as far as the Prince being missing goes. This is a major security issue for our system and all other assignments are to be put on hold. Tamara and Dom proceed to the planet, you have an interview with the King at 1400 hours; Karl and Sarah find out all you can from this end, and we'll all meet back here tomorrow same time. Don't come back without answers. Dismissed."

"This is magnificent! Dominic and Tamara arrived on planet Zenar before twelve o'clock, as the formal invitation they received specified they would be served the midday meal before being presented to the King.

"Have you ever seen such palaces?"

"No." Tamara was never impressed by anything or at least she never showed it.

"Welcome honoured guests. We will show you to your quarters."

  They had been met by a welcoming committee but it was the beauty and the obvious aristocracy of the lady speaking that caught Dominic s attention.

"Please follow me and if there is anything not to your satisfaction please do not hesitate to let me know. You each will have your own personal valet for your stay, please let him know of your requirements. There is nothing that we cannot obtain for you to make your stay to your satisfaction. Your meal will be served in the dining room in one hour and then you will meet with the King. Good day."

"Who was that?" Dominic asked his guide as they entered the lavish guest quarters.

"That was the queen. Queen Irisi. She always oversees our guests personally. She is meticulous and hand picks the domestic staff herself. These are your attendants, please let them know your requirements. They will take you to lunch when you are ready. Good day."

Lunch was a grand affair. There was a banquet of food served on an enormous table with numerous wait staff hurrying in and out but with only two guests to serve. Incredibly there were native dishes from each of the guests original planets as well as some they could not recognize.

"I think we should extend our stay Tamara." Dominic could hardly speak between sampling all the exotic dishes. "This mission could take longer than expected."

"May I remind you that the princes' life may be at stake? Not to mention the security of all our planets?" Tamara picked at the food as if even her own dishes were not good enough to eat.

"Do you always have to be so dramatic?" Dominic scowled at her before holding his stomach. "Did you try that octopus, it was delectable! I think I may have consumed more than one should at lunch."

"You'd better get cleaned up, it's nearly time." They both rose and withdrew to their own rooms to prepare to convene with the king.

Tamara and Dominic were led into a large conference room with an immense round table in its centre. The rooms walls were decorated as were the public halls spread across the palaces, with pictures of historical figures of the royal family and various statues and ornaments placed at various points on the tiled floors. All the walls and floors seemed to be constructed out of a sort of pale golden coloured stone that was polished to a shine that almost blinded and then gilded everywhere in gold. The round table and surrounding chairs were also made from the same preferred stone. It made for a lavish feast for the eyes and the scopious opulence was overwhelming.

King Ptah and Queen Irisi and some others were already sitting at the table when the two agents walked in. They were flanked by their minders and guards standing behind them and at the two entrances. Except for the king and queen, they were all dressed in a gold military uniform with stars and badges depicting the highest rankings. The group all stood as the two guests were ushered towards their allocated seats opposite them and it was quite intimidating to be received by such a large company of people. Even the usually self controlled Tamara looked a little on edge. But they quickly composed themselves and sat down.

Dominic was again struck by the incredible beauty of the queen sitting opposite him. She had long curled locks that ran all the way down her back of a rich auburn colour. Her skin seemed to glow with an iridescent sparkle of gold, which set off her bright green eyes to perfection.

The room became suddenly silent as the king began to speak. "We thank the Earth government for responding so swiftly to our request for assistance. You know Queen Irisi, and this is my nephew Lieutenant General Kahotep, my niece Lieutenant General Odjit, Major Generals of each Air Force team." He waved his hands at various individuals as he introduced them, of which there were up to ten seated at either side of him. He then motioned across to the other side of the table. "Special agents Tamara and Dominic Bellarto." Their introduction didn't sound quite as impressive, Dominic thought disparagingly.

Everyone nodded at each other.

"Please direct your attention to the screen." A hologram appeared in the centre of the table with an image of Prince Adabi.

"Father, I have arrived on planet Bosworth. I will let you know when discussions are concluded. Out."

"That was the last communication we received from him. That was 5 days ago. Negotiations are scheduled for one day only and all personnel, including my son, are to check in daily with their location. Of course we are a society that require the highest security measures due to our rare resource Krystal Gold, as you must know. These measures are strictly adhered to and upheld by the royal family. So you can understand how concerned we are that we have not heard from the prince and his unit."

"Did you say planet Bosworth?"

"Yes. Mr. Bosworth approached us recently about purchasing some large amounts of Krystal. Usually most negotiations are done on our planet but Mr. Bosworth insisted we let him extend his hospitality to the prince overnight. We agreed as Prince Adabi is an experienced traveller and he was accompanied by our Chief Security Officer, General Richter."

"That's trouble." Dominic shook his head. "Unfortunately there is not a lot known about Hugh Bosworth or how and where he came by his fortune, and we have recently had a disturbance on Earth with links to him."

"That is all we can say right now." Tamara gave Dominic one of her *looks*. "But what we can say is that if Prince Adabi has been delayed or is being held by Bosworth we will launch a full and immediate investigation and the full extent of the solar systems powers will be exercised. Has there been any other events lately out of the ordinary?"

"Yes. A few months ago two of our top scientists were

kidnapped and executed. We could not find out who the perpetrators were. They were held on an old solitary moon until Prince Adabi headed a rescue team, but Goblins had killed them before they could get to them."

"Please excuse us." Tamara stood up abruptly. "We must return to Earth now and begin the investigation. Rest assured that we will do everything possible to locate and potentially rescue your son. We will remain in constant contact with you and inform you of an update as soon as one arises. Thank you for your hospitality. Goodbye for now." Tamara was brisk and businesslike.

The Zenarian King decided that he had no choice but to leave the situation in Earth's' hands for now. He could think of no other options to get his precious son back. He nodded and Tamara left the room quickly, Dominic hastily rising from his seat and following her.

DEADLY EFFECTS

Sarah felt her head getting dizzy and excused herself from the meeting. She was annoyed and embarrassed because the meeting was in David Spencer's office and all the agents were in attendance.

Tamara and Dominic had just returned from the planet Zenar that morning and had come straight to the meeting at EI headquarters. Karl and Sarah had been researching the latest details about the planet and the royal family. Apparently there'd been some trouble recently with one of the air force lieutenants, a member of the royal family, briefly ending up in jail on the sea planet. There'd also been an incident where two of their eminent scientists had been kidnapped and murdered. "That planet has had a bit more of its fair share of activity lately." David was obviously pleased with their work. "What's the story with the Prince?"

Tamara answered, "We think he's being kept prisoner by Bosworth, perhaps for a ransom, and we also think Bosworth was involved in the murder of the two scientists."

"Bosworth again! What's that man up to I wonder. It might be connected with the findings in the desert then. How sure are you the prince is on Bosworth?"

Dominic joined in. "His last message was traced as coming from inside the planet. And the prince was there by invitation. He hasn't been seen or heard of since."

"Ok, Karl---------" David began to speak but Sarah interrupted him by jumping out of her chair.

"I'm sorry, I have to go!" Sarah rushed to the door holding her head.

"Serena what is it? I cant talk right now."

The female feline was obviously very distressed. Sarah could feel the intense fear emanating from her being.

"Sarah you have to help us! Look, this is the man who's hurting us!"

Sarah looked to where the cats gaze was fixed and unbelievably she saw Bosworth in front of her. In front of them. He drew towards them menacingly and peered closely into their faces.

"You two will do what I want you to do or you will both die, make no mistake!"

The cats snarled in response but the big man just chuckled which then turned into a sneer.

"You will kill the man I want you too and then you will be set free. You do want to be set free don't you? I personally guarantee you can go back to wherever it is you came from. How would you like that? You will kill him and you will do it today!" His voice raised sharply until he was shouting. "DO YOU UNDERSTAND!"

It was not a question. He then left the concrete pen that had become the cats home.

"You see Sarah? You have to do something, you have to get us out of here. Sarah are you there?"

Sarah's' head was spinning. Suddenly she knew how Bosworth planned to kill Prince Adabi Zenar and make it look like an accident. But how could she tell El what she knew? They would laugh at her, it would completely destroy the thin bit of credibility she had.

"Sarah, are you there?!" The urgency in Serena's' voice was unmistakeable.

"Yes, yes I hear you. I'll help you, don't worry." Somehow she had to make her boss understand.

"I'm really sorry, I had to leave for a minute." Sarah went back into David Spencer's' office to see an ugly smirk on Karl s' face. She realised it was very hard for him to look ugly so he must be really annoyed. David was annoyed too, but he went on speaking as though Sarah had never left the room.

"So, Karl you and Sarah face the SS8 council representatives this afternoon to obtain permission to enter planet Bosworth and rescue the prince, and you two get your report ready to present to council about the mine here. Any questions?"

"We don't have time for that!" As soon as Sarah said it she became scared; contradicting the head of Earth Intelligence wasn't something you did every day, but she knew time was running out for the prince and she had to let them know. Everyone looked at her in surprise.

"Look, I know something. And time is running out for the prince. We have to get him out of there today!"

"Well, what is it you think you know?" Karl asked sarcastically.

"It's a bit hard to explain but here goes. Do you remember the news article a few months ago about an exotic and rare species of felines that went missing from a collector?"

"Yes, they're still missing, go on."

"Well I know where they are."

"Well that's wonderful Sarah, now can we get back to saving the prince?" Karl was losing his patience.

"No, no, Karl, hear her out." Surprisingly to Sarah, David seemed to be listening to her.

"They're on planet Bosworth and he's training them to kill Prince Zenar and make it look like an accident!" Sarah blurted it out quickly before she lost her nerve.

"How do you know this Sarah?"

"I can hear their thoughts." Sarah looked down sheepishly. She was sure they were going to throw her out of the building.

"Who's' thoughts, Sarah?"

"The cats, the ones that went missing."

"Oh now we've heard everything!" Karl had heard enough and

got up to leave. "Do we have to listen to this David? Come on."

"That's enough Karl. Sarah, how long have you known about the cats?" David seemed to believe her.

"That they were on Bosworth? Only today. But I've been talking to them for a long time now, months."

"You know Sarah, I've been waiting for you to confirm this, that you can talk to these animal species, and now that you have, this will make it so much easier to infiltrate Bosworth and save both the felines and the Prince."

Karl looked incredulous. "You knew about this?" He and Sarah said it in unison.

"Yes, actually, I did and I'm sorry that I had to keep it a secret from all of you,
especially you Sarah. We'd been tracking contact between the cats and an unknown party on earth for a while but then the contact became more frequent and we wanted to know why. We also needed to know if that person was involved with the abduction of the cats. You see simply talking can be detected by a certain wavelength but it just so happens that thoughts and other types of telepathy are on a slightly different frequency and its been a policy of EI to track the different wavelengths for some time now. So Karl, now you know why we needed to get Sarah up to speed so quickly. She is the unknown party, and yes, she can communicate with certain species of intelligent animate beings. In fact some species do not use speech at all. So Sarah please fill us in on what you know."

"The Zenarians insist on including their men on any

contingent and we can't really stop them from doing so." Karl and Sarah were in David's' office getting their final instructions for the rescue mission to planet Bosworth. David was agitated and Sarah was beginning to recognise his moods. When he was being very serious as he was now, he would lean with both hands over his desk, looking intently at the papers spread haphazardly across it and avoid eye contact altogether. It was then that you knew there was no manoeuvring on that assignment.

"I don't need to remind you of what rests on this situation. It threatens the stability of the whole solar system as well as our reputation for security around all the galaxies. Karl I leave Sarah in your capable hands. You will rendezvous with the Zenarian forces on planet Bosworths' fourth moon Sinope. Dismissed."

Karl and Sarah stood next to each of their space ships. "You know what to do? You're on your own now but I'll always be right behind you even if you don't know I'm there. Check your ear piece. Can you hear me?" This was a side of Karl Sarah had never seen before. A kind and caring side. She was just wondering if he could be faking it when he put his hands on her shoulders and looked straight into her eyes.

"Look I may not have been fair to you and I'm sorry, but I want you to know right now that I've got your back ok?" With that he gave her shoulders a tug and got into his ship. "Can you hear me? We're a team, remember that." And he flew off.

She hurriedly got into hers and followed.

THE DEADLY MISSION

Sarah had done weeks of intense training on the simulator of the combat air striker she now sat in, under Karls expert guidance, but it was still exciting to be in the real thing. Even though it was set on autopilot for the ten minute trip to Bosworths moon, Sinope, she played with the insignificant switches like the aircon, switching it on and off, and the camouflage adjustor.

Karl shook his head and smiled as he watched her ship change from army green to yellow and then to pink. "Nice colour, girl." He was surprised at how contrite he felt for the way he had spoken to her, she really was a very sweet girl, and actually had impressed even David at how quickly she had picked up everything.

"As soon as we get close to Sinopes orbit don't forget to change to cloaking."

"I wont." Sarah felt chuffed. She was on a space combat ship and she was having fun! But she was immediately brought back to reality when she saw the Zenarians impressive ships hovering just outside Sinopes' perimeter. They too immediately converted to cloak and everyone was invisible.

Karl and Kahotep were old buddies.

"Hey dude, long time!" Sarah could hear the delight in the strangers voice.

"You've been up to no good as usual Kaho!" Karl was obviously glad to meet his friend again too.

"Never! Is there anything you don't know?" Then their friend got right down to business. "Any changes to the plan?"

"No. You ready to cause a disturbance while we sneak in, take a look around? We'll let you know if we need you."

"Right on, lets go!"

Sarah could see the blips of her and Karls and the ten ships
of the Zenarians on her screen but she knew that they were all
invisible to anyone else, visually or electronically. They slipped
in to planet Bosworth and looked for a place to land. They saw
a building that seemed to stand out from the rest of the old
factories that dotted the landscape, and they headed for that
one.

Karl saw the landing platform on the roof but directed his ship
to one that was three buildings further on.

He waited for Sarah to join him on the roof.

"We'll go on foot from here. This way." He glanced at the
visual guider in his hand that gave him a picture of everything
ten metres in a circle from where he was standing.

"Sarah, you're close!" Serena had sensed Sarah nearby.

"It's the cats! I'm coming to get you now!"

"It's too late! They're taking us to the prince and they have a
mind control device. When they turn it on we don't know
what's happening and they control us. What should we do?!"

Sarah and Karl were now at the corner of the tall building.

"I see them. Here you take this." Karl handed her the guider.

"Get them out of here, don't wait for me, I'll get the prince."

They were now inside the building which was eerily quiet.
Suddenly they heard a huge explosion and the entrance came
alive. Men from the planet Thuran and many goblins appeared
from lifts and doors and ran outside. Karl and Sarah hurried
inside the lift.

"The cats are on the same floor as the prince. We have to
hurry."

Sarah felt a pain in her head. "They're using the mind control
device on the cats. I'll try to counteract it. It's instructing them
to attack the prince. They're nearly at the door to his room."

"You can do it Sarah. Just a little bit longer and we'll be there.

Come on lift, hurry up!" But it was only seconds till it stopped.
The lift doors opened and they ran towards a doorway
opening straight in front of them, at the end of the hallway.

They could hear snarling inside the room as they entered but
nothing could prepare them for the sight of the lion size but
elegant cats standing over a man at the other end of the room.

Bosworths right hand man, Fragar, stood behind pointing a
device at the cats. He turned, surprised at the intrusion, but
quickly pulled his gun from its holster hanging around his hips
while shoving the device into one of his pockets.
Karl was too quick for him though, and leapt on him, pinning
him to the ground while the laser gun spun away, out of reach.
"Stop those cats!", he yelled.

Sarah stood behind, amazed to see the cats in the flesh. She
knew they were helpless and she began to concentrate her
mind the way Dargon had trained her to do.
"Dargon! Serena! Control and block! Control and block!" She
shut her eyes and directed her thoughts to the cats minds.
She looked up but they were still advancing on the prince.

Karl and Fragar were still fighting in the background so she
had to stop them herself.

She closed her eyes again and concentrated her thoughts
again. "Control. Control your minds. Dargon. Serena. Listen to
me, Sarah. Block. Block the device. CONTROL AND BLOCK!"

The cats shook their heads and looked around. They then
realised where they were and backed away from the prince.
Fragar saw them and knew it was over and took the
opportunity to run out and enter the lift. He laughed as the
doors closed behind him.
"Well done. I'll take the prince to Kahotep and you get the cats
back to safety on Earth. I'm going after him."
The prince stood up. "I'm coming too. I'm going to enjoy
flattening that bastard!" And they knew he meant it.

The two men ran to the lift, jabbing at the button, then rushed through the stairway door.

Sarah ran to Serena and embraced her.

"Well done indeed!" Dargon was not one usually ready with appraisal but this time he was sincere. "Thank you Sarah, I could not have asked for more from you."

"You're welcome Dargon, I had a good teacher. Now lets get you two to safety."

They walked towards the lift as the doors opened for them.

Karl and Prince Adabi ran out of the entrance doors and straight into Kahotep and Odjit.

"Adabi, are you alright!?" Kaho flung his arms around his cousin and gave him a big squeeze. "You scared us man, not to mention the good old king!"

"I'm good thanks to all of you. It was my mistake, I shouldn't have come here. Has anyone seen or heard from Richter?"

"No, we're just about to start a search. And there goes Fragar and his men!"

They all looked up as a bevy of ships rose into the air and vanished into the stratosphere.

"Let them go. We better get the prince back."

Just then the Zenarians brought Richter and the other prisoners to them.

"Found them locked in an old factory. He's ok," Qeb explained. "The Thurans and the goblins had decrepit old ships. They ran pretty quickly after they saw us."

"I'm so sorry I left you alone Prince, I take full responsibility." Richter was mortified at what had happened.

"No one could have foreseen this Richter. Luckily we had old Kaho and Odjit, not to
mention the Earth's finest at our disposal." The prince patted him on the back. "I'm just glad we're all ok."

Karl wanted to leave the planet. "So let's go back to Earth and see if we can locate Bosworth. He's in a lot of trouble."

"Sure, but there's one more thing we have to do. When I came to the planet I saw an artificial atmosphere with some white ladies inside whom I'm sure were also being held prisoner. Can we find them?"

"Ok we'll spread out. I'm sorry Prince but you have to stay with me until I can officially release you. Everyone else back to their ships. Anyone see anything, call out." And Karl directed the prince towards his ship.

The fleet of ships travelled slowly around the perimeter of the planet until they came across a huge clear white bubble on the other side. Inside the bubble it was snowing and everyone looking gasped in amazement. They could see numbers of women all dressed in white gowns with flowing white hair floating around inside.

"How do we get in?" The prince asked.

"It must be controlled remotely, we'll have to find the control room. It's probably back at the main building."

"I'm on it." Kahotep flew back in the direction they'd come from.

"Ok, I can see an entrance on the south side of the bubble invisible to the naked eye but I can see it here on the screen. I'll set it to open, it should start flashing."

Kahotep was in the control room. "It's quite a set-up in here, you gotta see it Karl."

"Thanks, we will. There it is. The prince and I will go in, everyone else prepare to return to Earth."

Karl parked his ship outside what he could now see was an entrance way that flashed as a coloured door into the bubble.

Inside the bubble it was snowing and they were freezing. Two women came towards them and Adabi recognised the younger one as the girl he had seen when he first arrived on the planet.

"I am Queen Yoroni and this is my daughter Princess Yasmini.

I hope you are here to free us. We have been locked up by Bosworth for a long time."

"Yes we are. I am Karl Harper from planet Earth, and this is Prince Adabi of the planet Zenar. We will order a ship immediately to take you back to your planet. Which is your planet and do you know why he took you prisoner.?"

"Thank you. We are from the planet Snow in solar system 6. As you can see our race can only survive in very low temperatures and your ship must reflect that. Our planet has a vast resource of clear diamonds and he was holding us to ransom. I don't know the outcome of the extortion on our planet. We have had no contact with the outside world at all."

"How long have you been here?"

"For four years."

"I'm so sorry to hear that. We must find out what has happened to your planet before we can send you back there. Would you mind staying on Earth until then? We will provide a comfortable suitable compound for you if you agree."

"Thank you, that would be wise."

"Good, I'll send for a ship immediately."

THE EARTH, A SANCTUARY

Back on Earth, Sarah was spending time getting to know the cats in person. In the beginning she had to consciously stop herself from saying the words and just thinking them instead, the eerie silence enhancing the unnatural act of not talking. But after a while she found it an efficient thing to do, because she could continue an activity and not have to enact the physical exertion of talking. She hadn't realised before how much energy people used just to talk. The thing she didn't pick up straight away though, were the nuances in thinking that were so obvious when someone spoke, by the tone of their voice or the slant of the head, or even a pursed lip.

"So what happens to us now?" Even though the cats were now safe and secure here on Earth, Dargon did not seem to be relaxing.

"The earth has applied to the galaxy council to take control and occupy your original planet and if successful you'll be transported back there. Isn't that wonderful?"

Serena and Dargon exchanged looks.

"Am I missing something here? That is what you want isn't it? To go back to your planet and see who's still left of your family etcetera? I know there's something you're not telling me, I could feel it since you first told me about how you were taken. Now what is it? You must know you can trust me with anything by now."

"We have to tell her Dargon." Serena turned to Sarah with the most woeful look on her face. "When we were being captured we handed our baby, the only baby we can ever have, over to her uncle who took her down into underground caverns made by the smaller animals who lived below the ground. We don't know what happened to her. I'm sorry we didn't tell you before but you can see why we don't trust other species."

Sarah couldn't look at the cats. She knew from her research that Quatar had been completely destroyed by fire and that all the intelligent animals had been captured and hence disappeared into other worlds. But the cats were very intuitive and could sense her hesitation.

"You know something don't you, Sarah. You must tell us."

"Tell us now, Sarah. We have to know."

Now she realised why Dargon was always agitated.

"Maybe it's better that you see for yourself. Just watch the screen over there and I'll bring it up." " Computer show history of Quatar in video mode."

The screen showed images of animals being captured and taken up into spaceships, and then showed vivid pictures of the planet being consumed by a fire that covered the whole planet, and from a distance looked like a burning sun. It then showed images of the scorched planet once the fire had burned out with no life visible at all.

Serena took a huge gasp at the sight of the planet burning and then began to weep. Sarah saw Dargon's shoulders fall and his head slump as he realised the devastation that had befallen their planet.

"I'm so sorry. I just couldn't tell you earlier but I didn't know about your baby. It's unlikely there were any survivors on the planet. The temperature of the fire was recorded as heating the nearby planets for weeks. Look, I'll type in your species and see what comes up. Maybe there are survivors like yourselves on other planets. The problem we face is that you were all captured illegally and it remains illegal on all our solar systems to harbour animals from your planet, so it's all gone underground. But we'll see what the computer comes up with. It could take a while."

"So you two know each other?" Adabi realised that Kahotep and Karl were friends.

Since coming back to Earth Karl had been appointed Adabi's guard and chaperone, while Richter and his men travelled back to Zenar to report to the King. After some much needed rest, he had been showing the three cousins the sights. The group were sitting in a restaurant and Adabi realised Kahotep had met his match as far as being a hooligan was concerned. The two friends had been drinking and joking all night and had started talking about their past endeavours.

"So you knew each other before this happened? How can that be?"

"Oh we've met here and there." Kaho and Odjit looked at each other.

"What doya mean, we've been around the galaxy together for years now Kaho?!" Karl was beginning to slur his speech after challenging Kaho to a few too many shots of whiskey.

"For years? What does he mean, cousin?"

"Nothin, nothin, he's talking rubbish, he's just drunk. I'm going to the loo." He fell off his chair and stumbled off.

Adabi looked at Odjit. "Did you know about this Odjy?"

"Lighten up cos, we've been going out for years. Did you expect us to stay cooped up on that archaic planet?"

"You were going out too? Without telling me?"

"Well you are the prince and a bit uptight lately darlin'."

"But how? Didn't security find out?"

"Of course they know, it's a well known secret. Everyone does it. Sorry cos."

Adabi's obvious shock and dismay sobered up Karl and he decided maybe they'd had enough for one day.

"I think we better turn in. I've got a meeting tomorrow with my superior, and we've got council on Friday."

"I'll wait for Kaho, you two go ahead. Don't be mad dabby, we just didn't want to get you in trouble." But Odjit couldn't appease Adabi and he couldn't help feeling troubled by the news that Zenarians had been travelling without the royal families knowledge for some time. But he couldn't help his natural inclination of always protecting Odjit.

"It's not your fault, Odjy. But tell Kaho I want to hear all about it tomorrow. And the truth this time."

Sarah and Karl were in David Spencer's' office. He was alternately one minute circling the room and the next standing with his hands on his desk, and Sarah could almost tell what he was thinking by his actions. On one hand he was pleased with the success of the rescue and on the other hand he was worried about something else.

"Well done to both of you. I couldn't have asked for a better outcome. The Zenarian

King is thrilled and has invited you both to a ceremony on his planet to thank you. We still have a few problems though. At council on Friday I expect a release to be granted to return the prince officially to Zenar and you will both accompany him and return him to the sanctity of his relatives. Also at council we begin the enquiry into the state of the cats planet Quatar and the release of the cats. We also have the outcome of the decision on the ownership of the mine. My connections tell me we will be granted ownership as all resources belong to the planet they are found on; and a warrant will be put out for Bosworths arrest. His planet has been compounded to the councils ownership. We are also making enquiries about the state of the Snow planet. How are the cats holding up Sarah?"

"They're good under the circumstances sir."

"Good. Any questions?"

"No sir." Sarah and Karl left his office.

"Karl, wait up." Sarah ran after Karl who was disappearing

down the hall. "Listen I was wondering if you could help me. The cats apparently had a baby just before they were captured and they're wondering how to find out if any other of their species survived? How do I go about doing that?"
"Okay. Leave it to me and I'll look into it. By the way I'm taking the royals out for a drink tonight, would you like to join us? Sort of celebration drink, what do you think?" Sarah thought he seemed momentarily nervous.
"Sure, love to."
"Ok, pick you up at five."
"Great." But he had already walked off.

  Sarah was astonished at the way Karl and Kahotep were behaving. No one watching would have guessed that they were an agent and a member of a royal family respectively. They were drinking excessively and goading each other and it seemed they'd done it many times before. Their exaggerated stories of their individual heroics were taking on monstrous proportions but their audience realised some of it must be true.
"So you've been on missions together?" Sarah wasn't the only one intrigued by their stories, Adabi wanted to know more.
"We'll tell you when Kaho can stop boasting." Odjit was suddenly feeling neglected with the beautiful blonde sitting opposite her and Adabi directing all his conversation in the young girls' direction.
" So Sarah, I'm so glad you could come tonight. I never got the chance to thank you for saving my life."
"Oh glad to be of service, I've never met a royal before." And a strikingly handsome one at that, she thought. "What's it like being a prince anyway? I hear your planet is lovely."
"People keep secrets from you." He looked at Odjit and smiled. "Well you'll see for yourself what our planet is like next week. You are coming aren't you?"

"Yes absolutely, can't wait. I just can't leave the cats for too long though. They sort of rely on me, you know."
"How are they holding up?"
"Good, but their location is confidential, they're still feeling like they're captives, but they are grateful. It's only till we sort out where they're going. It takes time."
Odjit was becoming bored with the inattention and changed the subject. "Where have you been hiding dabby?" She used the nickname when she was trying to get his attention. "I haven't seen you during the day at all."
"Actually I've been escorting the snow princess, Yasmini, around the planet. We've spent some lovely days together, she really is a sweet girl."
"Oh have you." Odjit became really annoyed at the princes' disclosure. "I thought they couldn't live without their precious snow."
"Apparently they can leave their environment for short periods of time. They're also joining us on Zenar next week. The king has agreed to build a compound for them to stay on our planet until their situation is sorted. It is the least we can do for them."
"I thought the Earth was looking after them."
"They were but I made a formal request for them to remain on Zenar while they wait for an outcome. It will be made official at the council on Friday but its been accepted, after Queen Yoroni agreed of course. I've gotten to know them quite well. They're a lovely gentle people."
Odjit had heard enough. "I'm going to bed." And with that she left.

Karl and Prince Adabi attended the council meeting of Solar System 8 on the Friday and everything transpired as expected.
Plans were finalised to transfer the snow people to Zenar and Karl and Sarah were to accompany them.

As Odjit decided to stay in her room the last night, the four friends, Karl, Kaho, Adabi and Sarah, met for a final dinner on Earth before preparing to depart for planet Zenar the next day.

As the others left and Karl walked her home, Sarah realised she may have been wrong about the way she thought of Karl. He took his work very seriously, but now she knew he could be a lot of fun as well.

He was about to leave her at her door, when she turned around.

"Wait Karl, I forgot to give you this back." And she handed him his fathers pen.

"My pen, I thought I lost it, thank you!" And he kissed her on the cheek impulsively.

She put her hand on her face where he had kissed it and watched him skip away. She flushed at the thought and then checked herself. Stop being silly, she thought. But the feeling lingered.

THE FUGITIVES

Bosworth was a seasoned traveller and an accomplished criminal across many galaxies, and therefore knew of the countless empty moons and accommodating planets that provided a safe haven and a welcome escape route whenever he required them.

He didn't intend on travelling too far from solar system 8 just yet though, not with that new find of the mine of Krystal Gold on Earth, a mine which just happened to belong to him. Or so he thought.

He'd been sloppy and underestimated the tenacity of the people on that small planet and their friends the Zenarians, together a rich and powerful force in the galaxy. But he was new to this part of the universe and it was time to get to know this part of the world a bit better. Usually he preferred to work alone but sometimes friends came in handy, especially those that had a beef with his enemies. And with a planet that threw it's weight around like Earth obviously did, there had to be someone out there feeling a bit like he did. Cheated. It was time to make some new friends.

"Fragar! Get the gobs in here. Lets see what they know about this galaxy and who lives around here."

"Hhh." Fragar just grunted and left. Bosworth didn't trust the guy, he didn't trust anyone, and sometimes he wondered why Fragar hung around, but there were millions of vagabonds, petty criminals with no ties to any particular region or system, hanging around the universe, and he was easily replaceable if the need ever arose. But he seemed loyal so far, and that was a trait that was hard to find in his line of business.

The noisy grumbling of the goblins preceded their arrival from beyond the dilapidated rooms of a deserted hotel on the deserted planet Bosworth had fled to.

"Shut up!" Bosworth yelled at the first sight of them as they wrestled through the small opening of the door and shoved eachother to try and be the first into the room. He hated the ugly little weazels but they came in useful, readily sharing little titbits of gossip for small rewards like food, or fuel to travel on their broken down ships. They were things Bosworth could easily provide and so he tolerated their annoying presence for the inside knowledge they somehow acquired about the local patronage.

"So Bort, what can you tell me about those Earth dogs? And keep still!" The goblins were always shuffling from one foot to the other and grumbling under their breath. The ugliest and the bulkiest one named Bort, seemed to be the leader, although in the Goblin world you could be usurped at any time if you didn't keep your guard up and you didn't watch your back.

But Smuz sputtered up first and jumped from side to side, pushing his cohort behind him. "I know something!", he said excitedly, spit flinging from his mouth.

"Well, out with it!" Bosworth could only stand being in their company for a short time.

"Earth are running out of gas supplies and looking for other places to get it."

"Gas, you say. That could come in handy. What else?"

But Bort wasn't to be outdone and shoved Smuz out of the way. "Earth Intelligence are-a pushing around ha-some of the other solar ha-systems trying to get them all to ha-join into one. Ha-ha-most are agreeing, but there's one ha-resisting-ha." His sentences were punctuated with small grunts making them nearly impossible to understand.

"Translate Fragar!" Bosworth was becoming increasingly

agitated with the goblins' frenetic disposition, but he knew he needed to keep them on side, so he yelled at Fragar in frustration. "What the hell is he trying to say?!" He turned away in disgust, careful to hide his loathing.

Fragar knew when to step in and keep the peace. He was sure these stupid little squealers had no idea the danger they were in and they needed their information at the moment. He moved in between his boss and the informers and waved to them to keep back. He turned towards his boss. "There's a planet in one of the other solar systems that is resisting the galaxies council to merge into one. Its called Gaule and they are a small belligerent group of people with a large weapons program."

"Now that's what I'm looking for. People with a bit of backbone in their blood! Good work, now get out all of ya! And Fragar, get me some contacts on Gaule." He waved his hand at the door.

"And get us some food! I'm hungry!"

THE PRINCE AND THE PRINCESS

Sarah could not believe how her life had changed so much. She was an EI agent zooming around in fighter ships and travelling to different planets and meeting the most fabulous people. It was a shame she couldn't share her exciting stories with her friends and family, as her identity had to be kept a secret, but it was just so amazing.

The group had arrived on Planet Zenar and she could not believe the opulence before her eyes. Gigantic golden castles set against a background of a golden sea and golden sun drenched sky, it was a sight to behold. And inside the castles golden marble, gilded with pure gold and inlays of precious stones; murals, portraits and statues of generations of the royal family of Zenar placed throughout the buildings and long hallways.

As soon as they arrived Prince Adabi took on a different countenance, immediately transforming into the prince of his planet. Sarah had only seen him as the affable, always polite gentleman who sat next to her at the dinner table in a restaurant on Earth, but here he was a different man. He was the royal that all his subjects revered to and stared at as he walked past; and the children annoyed him, pulling on his clothes and following him everywhere, chattering at him trying to get his attention, right up until he entered the doors of the royal families great castle. Here he was the one that was always going to meetings with various people and no-one saw him again until the day of the ceremony, in her and Karl s honour three days later.

She didn't see Karl hardly at all either except for when they happened to be having a meal at the same time in the grand food hall that was always an extravagant banquet spread across two long tables that was automatically kept at the perfect temperature for serving with the latest technology built into the tables surface. The kitchen staff were constantly bustling in and out from the kitchen to the hall, replenishing dishes and introducing new ones. The great food halls were apparently spread throughout the planet in public castles and everyone in that immediate vicinity came and ate together at the appointed time. Apparently everyone on the planet was on a roster system that covered every function that was required to keep the planet running, and the citizens could choose which of these they preferred to do. It was a well run system and every Zenarian was brought up expected to go to work for the good of the planet. From what Sarah could see it couldn't be working more efficiently.

But Sarah had no time to miss her friends, for on arrival Odjit had taken it upon herself to become Sarah's' personal minder and guide, delightfully showing off all the virtues of her planet. Sarah had thought she had been a bit stand-offish on Earth, but on Zenar the two girls had become firm friends. And as a guest of the royal family she was housed in the royal castle and treated to the luxuries within.

There were large spa and steam rooms with massage and beauty staff whom waited on her every whim; she had never felt so indulged and special.

The two days since they'd arrived had passed so quickly and today was the day of the ceremony where herself and Karl would be presented to the royal family and honoured for rescuing the Zenars' prince.

Odjit ran into Sarah's' bedroom obviously excited by the coming event. She drew
open the gilded curtains and the bright sunlight flooded the room. "Sarah! Wake up! It's the day of the ceremony!"

Sarah found it hard to sleep on Zenar as the planet had five suns rotating around it and therefore it had no dark and no night. She could never tell what time it was as there was always a faint glow coming through the windows behind the curtains.

"What time is it?"

"Six o'clock, come on, you must start preparing yourself."

"Six o'clock? You sound like Karl, too early!" And she pushed her head under the pillow.

"No, come on, get up!" And Odjit pulled the covers off her and tugged at her arm, pulling them both onto the floor. They both got up giggling.

But Odjit couldn't contain her excitement. "Today we'll have our breakfast in the beauty rooms but we shouldn't have too much, there'll be a huge banquet after the ceremony, we'll be eating and drinking all night! We must look our best, it will take hours to prepare ourselves and I have a surprise for you. We are going to give a special presentation tonight, you and me! Did you know that I'm a dancer Serz?" That had become Sarah's' nickname. "My teacher has devised a special dance just for you and me, and we will come on first tonight! Isn't that exciting?!" And she began to dance around the room.

"I can't dance! I'm hopeless." Sarah was horrified at the thought of dancing in front of the royal family and thousands of spectators.

"Oh nonsense, every girl can dance, weren't you taught as a young girl? In Zenar every person is taught all arts and crafts as well as the other fundamental necessities like language and mathematics, ugh! School goes on forever. Anyway my teacher can turn anyone into an expert in minutes. Karl's doing something too you know but it's a surprise as well. C'mon, no need to dress, straight to the baths!" And she dragged Sarah out the door.

Although the enormous courtyard was drenched in sunlight, massive spotlights had been placed at strategic points around the sides, producing a glaring spectacle that was blinding to the eyes. There were six gigantic flame torches at the four corners of the arena and at the sides of the throne area where the royals and distinguished guests were seated. The ceremony amphitheatre was a rectangular shape situated between two long underground buildings that housed the performers and some kitchens. Above the buildings were built rows of seats on each side of a performing area, which began at the entrances to the buildings in front of the thrones, and went for miles down to two large exits. The performers would firstly entertain the royals and honoured guests and then continue for hours down the long pathway to the end. Along the way they could stop at refreshment tables they shared with the public that had their own entrances to kitchens behind them, built into the side buildings.

Odjit said her goodbyes to Sarah and left her at one side of the entrance ways, as she had to take her place seated with the royal family on the dais. Sarah was left with her personal assistant that had been assigned to her on arrival, who explained how she would be presented to the King and Queen and then seated in the honoured guest area.

Sarah suddenly heard the sound of herald trumpets in a long and frightening salute to the King. This was followed by an urgent drumming, that then decreased to a constant low, slow, tone. She then heard some whistles and she was led out to the arena between two uniformed officers of the military. As she walked through the entrance door the fierce lights and the cymbals and trombones of the band set off and she jumped in shock. But she quickly composed herself at the sight of the royals sitting on the thrones to her left and she marched obediently behind the soldier in front of her. She had been dressed in gold attire reserved for esteemed visitors so that everyone knew to treat them with respect.

Ahead of her she saw Karl entering from the opposite entranceway, again accompanied by uniformed officers, and when they were both in the middle, the guards stood and faced the monarchs. Karl and Sarah did the same, if not a little slower. The auditorium was packed with thousands of onlookers and Sarah was shaking with fright but when she glanced at Karl he looked calm and attentive, so she pretended to be the same. The trumpets sounded again piercing and deafening, breaking the surprising silence of the air, and Prince Adabi stood up from beside his parents and walked down to them. Sarah could not see a microphone but his voice boomed through monitors spread the length of the amphitheatre and beyond.

"We stand here to honour the most important individuals ever to visit our planet, Planet Zenar. These two people single handedly are responsible for saving your Princes', Prince Adabi Zenars', life. This is a feat beyond compare and one that has never been experienced on this planet before.

These two foreigners have risked their own life to save the prince of your royal family and for this we bestow upon them our esteemed gratitude. Furthermore! As they have shown themselves to be more than friends or associates to the planet Zenar and its people by risking their own lives to save one of ours, we extend to them honorary citizenship to the Planet Zenar and eternal brotherhood to their originating planet, Planet Earth."

At this the crowd roared and Prince Adabi had to wait before he was able to continue. "To the planet Earth in return for their successful endowment of the means by which I stand before you again today, the planet Zenar pledge all military and resources support when requested. And now my fellow Zenarians! Let us honour our guests!"

The crowd roared again as the full force of the band filled the air with music and the sound was blaring. Sarah and Karl were led to their seats on the right side of the monarchies thrones and she could see Queen Yoroni and Princess Yasmini sitting on the other side. The seats immediately in front of the throne area on each side were filled with the high ranking officers of the military, and on the other side were seated what must have been important people in the community. The procession then began in front of them.

The military band in all its golden uniformed glory did a simultaneous turn and began marching down the golden carpet that led beyond the eye could see, lined with Zenarians clapping and cheering. They were followed by dancers and various entertainers which went on for hours.

Karl and Sarah were required to remain seated as the guests of honour beside the royal family but did so fascinated. They marvelled at a world that could put up such a fabulous demonstration. They were provided with delicious morsels of food and refreshments throughout the day. At the end of the parade, Adabi again stood in front of the crowd.
"We of the royal family thank you for putting on such a wonderful show for our guests. Now enjoy your night!"

The members of the royal family and Queen Yoroni then got up and left through an entrance behind the thrones. The group of young people all got up and gathered together chattering bout the events of the last few hours.
"Come on Sarah, we have to get ready for our surprise. See you inside!" Odjit pulled Sarah away.
"What happens now?"
"We have another ceremony for special guests only of the royal family, you know people in the army and whatever. That's who we're dancing for tonight. Lets have something to eat and then we'll get ready. We're in the Kings and Queens royal quarters tonight, it's beautiful in there. And afterwards it's

a big party!"
"I don't know if I can pull off the dancing, Odjy."
"Oh, you'll be fine, stop worrying. Lets go have a look at the room."
"Are we allowed to?"
"Sure, I'm family remember."
   When they walked in Sarah thought the room looked set up for a wedding. There was the head table where obviously the King and Queen sat with their family and guests and then there were other tables set along the walls with a dancing area in the middle. The tables were set with golden tablecloths and golden candles with the crystal glasses shining and reflecting the golden soft lighting.
"It's beautiful!"
"Told you. Now lets go get ready. This is where we'll be dancing. Wait till you see our costumes." And she ran out the door they'd entered through. Sarah followed and Odjits' excitement was catching.

   The older members of the royal family were seated with Queen Yoroni and Princess Yasmini and the generals of the military and their wives at the head table. Other important guests filled the other ten tables along each wall, and a band played music at the other end. Continuous courses of meals were delivered to the tables and various entertainers performed on the floor in front of them.
   Suddenly the music and lighting changed and everyone looked expectantly at the double doors that the performers used to enter. The doors flung open and four girls dressed in brightly coloured kaftans danced into the room and lay down on the floor before the royal table. They were followed by two more girls, one dressed in a white flowing kaftan and the other in a black one, with jewels through their hair and adorning their bodies. Sarah with the blonde hair was the white dancer

and Odjit in the black smiled at her, reassuringly. They swirled around the room until they came to a stop in front of the main table. They bowed down to the floor and then abruptly ran the length of the room doing a grand jete` at the other end and then another on the return. They circled the room alternatively chasing and running from each other in dance, pirouetting one after the other, until finally they fell in a heap together in the centre of the floor. The girls in the coloured gowns then fluttered around them, pretending to pick them up, and then they all danced back through the doors. The diners clapped appreciatively but the music changed again and straight through the doors came soldiers dressed in the golden military uniform with Adabi, Kahotep and Karl leading in the front row.

They marched to the table and stood in front of the King and Queen and saluted, before turning and marching the length of the hall. Two groups then split and marched along the length of the tables back again, before halting in the centre of the floor in two lines facing the main table. All the soldiers were holding vintage swords that were apparently used by their ancestors in wars long ago, and they began a demonstration of wielding them in time to the music. After this they did one more march around the room and then filed out in twos.

The diners clapped again and the music continued, while the young performers came in and took their seats at their table.

Karl and Kahotep sat down but Adabi walked over to the main table, kissed his mother and brought Princess Yasmini back with him. He pulled out her chair and motioned her to sit down.

"Aren't you the gentlemen?" Odjit was still excited from her dancing.

"You were fabulous Odjy, and you too, Sarah." Adabi answered.

"Thankyou, so were all you guys." Sarah had watched the boys marching, screened in the outer room.

Karl was impressed by Sarah's' dancing as well. "So not only can you save princes, you can also dance up a storm."

"And not only can you save princes but you can wield a sword, who knew?" Sarah said back.

Everyone laughed.

"You two make a great pair then. Dancing, swords, is there anything earthlings can't do?" Kaho nudged Karl in the side.

"So you all know Yasmini don't you?" Adabi looked around.

"Yes. So tell us about your planet, Yasmini. What's it like? Must be cold is it?" Karl asked her, in between a morsel of food.

"Yes this warm climate takes a bit of getting used to, but we're managing." Up close she had an exquisite face, with her pale blue eyes and translucent white skin. "But we're finding we can increase the length of our tolerance every day. It's quite ironic really. Being prisoners has released us from our planet. Strange, huh?"

Adabi answered, "They say all things happen for a reason, maybe it's true," and he gave her a wry smile.

Everyone nodded, they could see the glint in his eye and knew what he meant. The prince had fallen in love. It was plain to see.

BACK TO BUSINESS

The party was over on Zenar and Karl and Sarah were due back on Earth.

After Prince Adabi found out that Zenarians had been travelling to other planets without the royals knowledge and approval, he could not hide it from his father, the King, and they had since made the decision that their citizens would be allowed to travel out of the planet, but entry by foreigners would still be totally restricted except through approval procedures that were being newly put into place. Kahotep and Odjit, accompanied by Richter, were to travel with Karl and Sarah to Earth to observe their security procedures for visitors, and to prepare a combined party to travel to the Snow planet to find out what had transpired in the four years since their Queen and Princess had been captured.

They ate their last sumptuous breakfast and a departure ceremony was organised. Everything on planet Zenar had a ceremony attached to it and Sarah was beginning to feel like a celebrity. She was quite enjoying the attention but Karl, on the other hand, just wanted to get back to work.

This time though, the small group of departees were presented to the King and Queen in a closed, less formal reception inside the royal palace. Queen Yoroni was seated next to Queen Isiri and the two foreboding women were giggling like schoolgirls, much to the chagrin of the King. "For goodness sake, what are you two women cackling about?!"

Queen Isiri looked at Adabi and smiled. "Perhaps your son should tell you himself."

Adabi and Yasmini moved forward toward the King. "I would

like to take this opportunity to announce my engagement to Princess Yasmini, with the Queens' permission." And unlike Adabi, he blushed, and bowed towards their two mothers.
"My goodness, congratulations son! I had no idea." And the king left his chair and kissed first his son on both cheeks, and then his future daughter in law. "Welcome to the family, and you also Queen Yoroni, welcome to our family. We must celebrate, this is a momentous occasion!"
"Again! Must we father? I don't think we can cope with any more celebrations."
"Nonsense! The whole of Zenar will be thrilled. It's not every day my only son and the heir to the throne, becomes engaged. This will be the biggest carnival we've ever had. I must go and prepare. You will return for the event won't you?" And he looked at Karl and Sarah.
Karl spoke for both of them. "Of course, we wouldn't miss it."

There were a throng of onlookers standing behind a cordoned off area of the spaceship airport. They let out a big cheer as the group was led by Adabi towards the ships, ready for takeoff.
Sarah gave Adabi and Yasmini the biggest hugs.
"Congratulations again! I'm so happy for you both. You'll let us know when the wedding is won't you?"
"Of course we will, silly." Yasmini had really come out of her shell since her stay on Zenar. She let go of Sarah's' hand regrettably. She'd really become so fond of her new friends.
Karl was ready to go and always the diplomat, "Thankyou for being such wonderful hosts, we'll let you know when we're leaving for your planet Snow."
Kaho gave Adabi a hug. "Congrats man, married? Whew. Couldn't ask for a better couple. The people are gonna go wild. Have fun with it." And he slapped him hard on the back and waved to the crowd.

They entered the ship to the cheering of the crowd and headed back to Earth.

It was straight back to business on their arrival on Earth, and they were driven directly from the ship to the EI building.

Tamara and Dominic were already waiting in David Spencer's office when they walked in. The room seemed quite small this time, with Kahotep, Odjit and Richter joining the group.

David Spencer walked in without looking at them and they knew something was not good.

"My sources tell me that Snow in system 6 has become a closed planet. There's been no activity in or out for some time and the trade in diamonds has ceased. That tells me we could be in for trouble." He always spoke as if he himself were going on each mission.

"We are going in prepared for a fight. We don't think Bosworth has left our system so someone's there running the show for him. Karl, take your best men. Kahotep, Richter I'll leave it to you about what you want to do. Notify your superiors and let me know."

"Sarah about the cats. We've been to Quatar, it's sustainable again, the grass plains have replenished over the years, so you can return the cats. We've located some of their relatives, and other species that were taken illegally from the planet and they've been returned. Unfortunately not all of them could be located. We've done our best, tell them that. I understand you're accompanying Sarah, Odjit?"

Odjit nodded.

"Right. Tamara, Dominic, I want you on Bosworths tail. Find out where he is and what he's up to. Any questions? Dismissed."

Odjit looked back as they walked out. "Is he always like that?"

She was a little intimidated by the austere man.

"No he's actually really nice. To me anyway." Sarah had become quite fond of David and he always made sure she was comfortable with her work. "Now let me formally introduce you to the cats."

"Dargon, Serena, meet Odjit from the planet Zenar." Sarah waved her arm with a flourish in Odjits direction.

"I can hear them." Odjit remarked nonchalantly, as if it was not important.

"You can?" But Sarah was surprised. She did not know Odjit had the gift of telepathy.

"Yes, they think they have seen my kind before. On their planet when they were abducted."

"What? A Zenarian on Quatar? Impossible! I can't hear them saying that." Sarah was at once confused and delighted.

"Can you hear her?" She asked the cats.

"Yes. She is a very experienced telepath."

Sarah followed their lead and ceased to talk but she could not keep up with their conversation.

"Your kind were on our planet. Are you friendly or are you an enemy? Were you one who kidnaps?"

"No, I'm friendly, I wasn't there." Odjit was horrified that they would think such a thing and she was becoming nervous.

"They looked just like you, dark skin, dark hair." Dargon had risen and was beginning to slowly circle around Odjit, staring at her with his sharp green eyes.

Sarah realised what was happening and yelled at him.

"Dargon she is friendly! Get away from her, right now! May I remind you that you are a guest on our planet!" She hoped that would work, but if it didn't she would have been at a loss to stop him. Luckily he realised she was right and it was not his place to impugn the stranger, even if she was guilty of something. He sat back down, ashamed of his behaviour.

"I'm sorry, she just looked like those people, it brought it all back, the horror, the fear; I apologise." He walked up to Odjit and put his paw on her knee. "I am sorry, please excuse my rudeness."

Odjit drew back as he approached, but then realised he meant no harm. "Of course, it must have been horrific. So they were dark skinned. There are many races with dark skin, and purple skin like the Canovins, and white skin like the snow people, all colours actually."

"Yes, how ridiculous of me." Dargon retreated to the back of the room.

Serena came closer. "He's been feeling the stress. And the excitement of perhaps going back. I guess it's taking it's toll on him. It was hard for him to lose our only kitten, as it was on me."

"Well I have some good news." Sarah wanted to change the subject. She glanced at Dargon, sitting in the back, licking his front paw. "We're taking you back. Your planet has replenished itself and some animals have already been returned. Quatar is under the official protection of the Milky Way galaxy council. Of course not all planets have joined yet, but we have a powerful force with the ones that have. Isn't that wonderful news?"

"Did you hear that Dargon, we're going back. When? Did you find our baby?"

"Ah, no, I'm sorry but we have never been able to find any more of your species. We do know though, that a small number somehow survived the disaster on your planet, some of your relatives, we don't know who they are, but they are awaiting your arrival. We leave as soon as you're ready."

Dargon returned to their conversation. "We're ready now."

THE RETURN TO QUATAR

Sarah and Odjit had been allocated a military escort led by Richter, chief of security on planet Zenar, to accompany them to return the two abducted and endangered feline species to their original planet of Quatar.

Quatar was situated in Solar System 1, a region that was understood to be one of the oldest, perhaps even *the* oldest system in the Milky Way galaxy. It primarily consisted of a cluster of dead stars, some that were once perhaps viable planets but had long since extinguished all activity, whatever that may have been, and a huge quantity of lifeless moons orbiting dead planets in an endless dance of empty memories.

There were a few though, that had withstood the ravages of time and the perils of space, to remain triumphant in the battle to contain life.

One of these primeval planets was Quatar. It was a simple planet consisting of the basic requirements for simple life forms, mountains, rivers, beautiful lakes, and grass plains. It was an environment based on pure, freshwater, completely devoid of seas, a vista of green and blue; green fields and the blue water that supported them.

It was similar to Earth but whereas Earth had advanced with its human population, Quatar had coasted along at a slow pace, with intelligent animals taking many centuries to evolve.

And because the planets were similar, Earth had not found it difficult to replicate and replenish the grazing animals that had once abundantly roamed this vast prairie. The scientists involved were at once worried at what introducing new species that were similar but not exact gene matches to the previous inhabitants would do to the planet, but also hoping that a slight variation of introduced species may benefit a planet that was not advancing as quickly as its neighbours. Anyway they had no choice, as the attractive breeds were stolen and the grazing herds that were left were ultimately destroyed in the fire that ravaged the planet.

As David Spencer had said, they'd done their best. Locating stolen stock was almost impossible and the voluntary anonymous surrender of animals program, through local galaxy advertising, had had limited success, so basically the planet would have to reinvent itself. And life had proved itself to be brilliant at doing just that, with the billions of living planets and different species thriving throughout the galaxies.

The Earth scientists were deriving a secret satisfaction in giving Mother Nature a little boost in restarting this ecosystem on Quatar. And in doing so they also decided to relocate some of the otherwise extinct creatures that only survived in zoos and sanctuaries on Earth. It was a controversial decision that had many opponents but was ultimately approved in galaxy council. A monitoring team of environmental analysts were appointed to remain unobtrusively on the planet for a number of years and report on the recovery of the ecology and habitat.

Sarah and Odjit marvelled at the incredible beauty of an unspoilt planet on their arrival. It had been a long time since they had observed a planet that was unspoilt by the needs and desires of demanding advanced races, who had their food and accommodation requirements literally at their fingertips. There were oohs and aahs from all of the accompanying men on the crewships as they slowly encircled Quatar.

The rivers, lakes and streams glistened brightly against the breathtaking mountains behind them, and the sweeping plains were already dotted with an array of grazing animals.

On seeing their beloved home again, the two cats could not contain there excitement and ran around the ship in a burst of happy energy they had not felt for a long time. They could not wait to feel the grass again under their paws and run for miles unrestrained.

"Are we landing?!" Serena could wait no longer.

Sarah smiled at her. "We have to check in at the landing station, then you're free to go. One more minute, I promise." Seeing the cats happy for a change warmed her heart, and she wiped a tear from her eye. She looked away but Dargon had seen it.

He spoke up. "Sarah, you know we cannot thank you enough for what you have done for us. You have been on our side from the beginning and now that you've brought us home, I cannot describe how grateful we are to you. This could not have happened without you and your generous heart and we thank you." He looked away, embarrassed to also be touched by the moment.

But Serena felt no such thing. She ran over to Sarah and pushed her head against Sarahs'. "He's right. You have been wonderful and the best representation of other worlds that we could have found. We love you and are indebted to you. If there is anything we can ever do for you, please let us know. Prrrrrr."

Sarah was touched. "This is not goodbye you know, I'll come and visit, wont we Odjy?"

"Of course."

"My goodness, look at that." Dargon peered closer to the window.

They were approaching the landing area and a greeting party awaited them.

"Is that a cat like us?!" Dargon could not believe his eyes. "It is, it's your brother, Serena, and who is that with him? A young one, who could it be? Do you think it could be ....? Is it possible?"

Serena was shedding tears and pushing at the door. Sarah pushed the button and the door slid upward. Serena rushed out with Dargon right behind her. Sarah and Odjit ran after them.

Serena and Dargon greeted their relative with lots of rubbing bodies and loud purring, and then they stood back to admire the appearance of the young kitten standing beside him. Serena was delighted. "Who's this young beauty then, Gallon?"

"Mum? Dad? You don't recognise me? I don't recognise you either. But Gallon told me you were coming."

"Viola, is that really you?" Serena went up to the young cat and rubbed against her. "I can't believe you're alive, but how? I thought I'd never see you again. And you've grown, you were only a baby when we were taken. It's incredible, I'll never leave you again."

"It's ok, mum, Gallon saved me. Tell them Gallon." Serena saw that Viola gave Gallon a look of pure admiration and knew that her daughter had fallen in love. Perhaps they were already a couple, she thought. It was strange to see her daughter all grown up. She had missed so much.

The large muscular cat raised himself boldly as if he again was living the harrowing time. "When you handed Viola to me and saw that you'd been taken up into the airships, we retreated deep underground into the burrows that the smaller animals had dug as their homes. We weren't the only ones. Many types of animals had escaped underground and it was dog eat dog for a while, especially around the small holes of water that some of the tunnels led to. We learnt to live and hunt in there until the huge fire had extinguished, and then, like others who had survived, we emerged back up onto the smouldering planet. It was very difficult for all, but the grasses did begin to regrow and slowly the land revegetated. But there were not many animals for us to hunt and we have had to roam far and wide to eat, until recently when the humans brought many new animals for us to feed on. And now you are here, we too thought you were gone forever."

"Are there others, Ponee and Nehe and Leoni?" Serena looked around expectantly.

"No, I'm afraid not. Just us and you two."

"Just us? You mean we're the only ones left? It can't be true!" Serena was in tears again. Dargon came over to comfort her.

"Don't make this a sad time darling. We have our Viola back and that's all that matters." He too rubbed his head over his daughter.

"C'mon Gallon, show us the sites. It's been a long time." He turned to Sarah, as did Serena.

"Goodbye and good luck." She said. "We have set up a station here to monitor progress upon the planet and have put in place an impenetrable security system so
that what happened before will never happen again. If you need anything let the people know and they will call us. We will see you again." Sarah felt a big part of her life was coming to an end and a feeling of sadness and regret came over her, but she was happy for them.

The four cats turned and ran off together.

Sarah and Odjit spent a few more days enjoying the rare sights of the planet before they began their journey back to Earth and civilisation. Up in the airship, they took one more sweep around the planet and saw simple animals living as they had for hundreds of centuries, a simple hierarchy that was brilliant in it's invention and worked successfully through time without fail. And from this time forward there would be a planet that was protected in its simplicity, left to evolve without interruption or disturbance, or assault from the outside world.

The girls took one last look, energised by the experience of a virginal world, and then shot out into the stratosphere, towards home.

BATTLE ON SNOW

There were billions of planets and stars in the Milky Way alone, not to mention the other larger nearby galaxies, Andromeda and Triangulum. Some had advanced races that had mastered the art of travel and others were developing planets with various stages of evolution. Karl and Kahotep had never had any reason to venture beyond their own galaxy and hoped they never would have. The citizens of the Milky Way were enough trouble as it was.

Unfortunately others didn't share their stay at home attributes, and were intent on travelling as far as they could and attaining whatever gain they could in the process, and as a result of their illicit behaviour they needed to keep moving to avoid persecution.

Bosworth was one of these characters. He moved between galaxies continuously, evading authorities and extorting naïve or vulnerable people as he went, ignoring the destruction and heartbreak he left behind.

But now he thought he had become untouchable. With a band of followers attracted to his pillaged riches, they would perform his bidding and with an army of willing criminals his heists became bigger and more daring and now he was holding to ransom whole planets and resorting to murder. He had been clever though, in choosing his victims, relatively unknown and obscure planets, occupied by people who kept to themselves, and who perhaps had no security systems in place whatsoever, and were therefore more susceptible to his assaults. So as time wore on he became more brazen and bold, and perhaps more careless. He had begun to feel pompous and invincible, and with no one on his tail he had gotten away with it.

Until now. In choosing planet Zenar this time, and leaving behind a trail of murders, he had underestimated this part of the universe. He had been lucky until now; but his luck was about to run out.

It took Karl and Kahotep and their soldiers only half an hour to get across two systems to SS6, but it was taking a bit longer to locate the planet Snow, buried in the profusion of other stars. They could not just let the automated controls land them inside the planet, they needed the benefit of surprise, so they landed in the vicinity of Snow and were now slowly making their way towards it, manoeuvring around other stars.

All the ones they were passing looked dim and uninviting, the surfaces bleakly covered in craters.

"No wonder Bosworth chose this area of the universe, who'd want to live here?" Kahotep voluntarily ran a shiver across his shoulders.

"That's exactly why he chose this part of the universe. He's been clever though, hasn't he, choosing isolated planets with naïve populations. Still, who would have guessed there'd be a planet with a rich diamond resource out here? He must have done his homework. We really should check other resource rich planets to see if he's given them a visit but it would take years to check them all. Our best bet is to catch him and try to find out where else he's been. Look, there it is, it's white compared to the others, they're all a dull grey. Look alive men, we've arrived! Cloaking now."

Karl and Kahotep were in the large main battleship with a flotilla of fighters accompanying them. They all cloaked invisible as he said the word.

As soon as they slipped into the planet they saw a hive of activity. Container cars buzzed everywhere, but they seemed to have a purpose, travelling in opposite directions across the white sky. It wasn't hard for the boys to work out what was going on, especially when they saw that some of the cars were manned by green goblins. The others were being driven by male snowmen.

"I'll take a car, and see where they're heading. Everyone stay out of sight." Karl moved to the back of the large, though undetectable ship, and flew out a small aircar. He followed a mean looking goblin to where his container car hovered and then lowered into a loading bay attached to a warehouse. Karl parked next to the warehouse and sneaked inside. He saw boxes being loaded with raw diamonds and then the boxes being loaded onto the container cars. It was all automated but was being overseen by the white snowmen, who were themselves being overseen by Thurins.

"Thurins!" Karl thought. He had been unfortunate enough to have dealings with the thugs from the planet Thuran before, a distant planet on the very edge of the galaxy, with no natural resources of their own. And being such a backward civilisation with only their labour to exchange for the necessities of living, they had to be provided travel to and from the places they worked. They were thugs who tried to take more than they worked for and Karl had been required on more than one occasion to attend one of their host planets to mediate between them and their bosses. They were the perfect comrades in crime for Bosworth, they'd have no qualms about roaming the galaxies and extorting goods for their own gain.

They'd be counting their lucky stars to be plundering diamonds! He had to save the helpless snowmen. They appeared all but defeated and this had been going on for years. So that's where Bosworth was getting his wealth from. Karl was glad Adabi could not see his fiances' people like this. He had to get back to the ship.

But he felt something stick into his back. "So what do we

have here?" Karl recognised the low snarl of a Thurin. "A spy, no less. Turn around, spy!"

Karl raised his hands and turned to look the thief straight in the eyes.

"Well, well, an earthling." The Thurin spat on the ground. "Aren't we a long way from home. Meddling in other peoples business again, I'll bet. You and those goblins have a lot in common!", and he hit Karl over the head with the laser gun he was holding. Karl fell to the ground but bounced off it and into the stomach of his attacker. They rolled on the ground punching each other, neither able to get the upper hand. The Thurin and the Earthman were equally matched at about the same height, but the Thurin was of much bulkier build. They were a solid built race, and it was there one advantage in the workforce, able to manage heavy workloads much easier than races of smaller frame.

"You didn't think he'd come all that way alone do you? Get up thug!" Kahotep kicked the Thurin in the side. He slid off Karl and was about to get up off the ground when Kahotep poked a gun into his temple. "Don't move," he said quietly.

"Thanks." Karl got up. "They're moving the diamonds into storehouses and probably selling them in small quantities around the galaxy. Clever strategy really, too clever for Thurins and goblins. Where's ya boss, thug?"

By this time Kahotep had him up against the wall and was searching him for weapons.

"Nowhere I'd tell you morons, even if I knew."

"You know alright. Start walking."

The Thurin made to walk but lunged at Kahotep instead, so Karl pulled out his gun and shot him between the eyes. He fell to the floor dead.

"Whoa, good shot man. Favour returned!" Kahotep had a habit of slapping people on the back but Karl dodged him this time. Kaho didn't know his own strength.

Back in the main ship they devised a plan. They would shoot down all the cars that were driven by goblins and then see who emerged from the fracas. They started doing just that and the same old decrepit fighter ships they'd seen on Bosworths' moon came out piloted by the rest of the Thurins. And because they did not have any decloaking technology they could not see who was shooting at them. Amazingly on their hasty retreat from the planet, they shot down some goblins that got in their way.

Kahotep was disgusted. "They really are a vile people. Imagine shooting down your colleagues."

"They weren't colleagues. They were partners in crime. The goblins would have done the same. C'mon lets see who's left."

They uncloaked their ships and descended to the ground, where they rounded up the goblins that had been left behind. The goblins were taken captive into the larger ship to be imprisoned on a holding moon in SS8 for interrogation and ultimately trial. They were going away for a long time.

The Snowmen were at first surprised and confused, but then so grateful when they found out they were to be given back the control of their planet and their diamonds. Karl and Kahotep left behind some Zenarian military to set up security on the planet so that the people and their valuable industry would be kept safe from now on.

The Snowmen were even more excited to learn that their women folk had been rescued safe and well and would be returned to the planet straight away. They would restore and prepare the planet for their long awaited return. The men asked if the rescuers would stay and enjoy the hospitality of their grateful hosts but Karl and Kahotep and their men declined politely. It was too cold! The snow had begun to fall again and they said their goodbyes and hurried to their ships.

They would detour to the Beach planet on the way home.

TROUBLE IN PARADISE

The two girls and the two boys arranged a rendezvous to meet Adabi and his fiance, Yasmini, on the beach planet.

Yasmini's mother, Queen Yoroni, and the other women and girls that had been taken prisoner on Snow, were now returning, but Yasmini was travelling with a Zenarian entourage, fitting for a future princess of one of the richest planets in the galaxy.

Although reluctant, Adabi agreed to meet Kahotep briefly en route to Snow, to give Queen Yoroni time to re-establish her planet, and to prepare for the noble guests.

The Beach planet was another popular resort destination, but was reserved for the mega-rich, frequented by the highest echelons of society, and entry by approved membership only. Karl and Kahotep were of course, members, and knew the resort and all its attractions well.

Kahotep had arranged with Richter for him to proceed back to Zenar first, and Kahotep would return to Earth with Karl to await further developments in the Bosworth case. It was a perfect arrangement that allowed the boys to sneak aside for a quick detour on the way home.

When Sarah and Odjit arrived, the two young men had already been at the resort for a couple of days. They were looking relaxed and cheerful on the beach, but Sarah was feeling sad about the departure of the cats, and was concerned about her role now as an agent. After all her assignment was now at an end, and perhaps El may not have any more need for her. She conveyed her apprehensions to Odjit on the trip over, who urged her to talk to Karl about it. But

when she saw him, all of a sudden Sarah was feeling inferior
and useless again, and she knew first-hand how
condescending Karl could be. So when she saw the boys
looking so carefree, she became annoyed.
"Hey girls, so good to see you, glad you could make it!"
Kahotep was always the charmer, and imminently ready for
party mode, but he seemed genuinely glad to see them. He
kissed them both on each cheek and gave them a hug.
   Karl smiled but didn't get up. "Hi girls, come over." He waved
his arm but didn't look up from behind his hat and sunglasses.
"Check in ok?"
   The girls laid their bags and towels next to the lounge chairs
and sat down. Sarah looked at the crystal clear aqua sea
spread out in front of her. It was a magnificent sight. People
were swimming and snorkelling, enjoying the perpetual warm
weather. The Beach planet was another with no weather
changes at all. Just beautiful warm sunshine every day.
"Yes, thank you, they knew who you were straight away. So
this is where all our taxes go." Sarah couldn't help her sombre
mood.
Karl heard it in her voice and sat up. He took off his
sunglasses and looked at her.
"What's wrong? Did everything go ok?"
She was taken aback with his abrupt concern. She hadn't
expected it. Perhaps he had really changed.
"Yes, just missing them I guess." She didn't trust him enough
to express her real concerns.
"That's understandable, but you can go and visit them."
"Not on my salary at the zoo I cant."
Karl laughed; now he understood. "Is that what you think?
That we just use you and then discard you again? Oh Sarah,
you're always so silly but in a sweet way." He then surprised
her even more by getting up and giving her a hug. "Do you
know how important you are to El? There aren't many who

have the *gift*, and even if you didn't, EI do not recruit lightly.
There must be something special about you. So stop worrying,
I'm afraid you're lion taming days are not over yet."
"See!" Odjit pinched her on the arm and looked at Karl. "She
was really worried."
"Well, after what we've all been through the last few months,
we deserve a holiday, so enjoy it." And Karl lay back down and
put his hat over his face.

   The four friends had been enjoying their holiday for a week
by the time the Prince and the Princess arrived.
   They were relaxing on the beach where they'd spent most of
their time, when they heard the sound of a commotion from
the hotel. They were about to go and have a look for the
cause, when they saw Adabi, Yasmini and all their minders
appear on the beach.
"My goodness, you know how to make an entrance!" Karl was
the first to stand up and greet them both with a hug. Kaho and
Odjit did the same, used to the constant presence of the
escort that accompanied Adabi everywhere he went. Sarah
though, felt slightly apprehensive at the large group standing
before her, but that feeling soon dissipated when Yasmini ran
over and hugged her.
"Oh, Sarah, I've missed you!"
"Me too." She squeezed her fondly back.
"Couldn't leave them home this time, I'm afraid." Adabi
laughed, happy to see his cousin and close friends again.
"We're only here for two days, we're expected on Snow by
Monday, but it's great to see you. Karl thank you for your help
on Snow, and Kaho, I've heard you were exceptional. Zenar is
waiting to honour you on your return. Thank you both."
Kahotep shook his head. Another celebration. "No doubt," he
said. "Enough Cos. Now lets enjoy our holiday."

   It seemed Adabi and Yasmini left as quickly as they had

arrived, and the others had only a couple more days left before they too had to leave for home.

It was noticeably quieter with the whole company gone, and the four were feeling just about ready to leave.

Kaho was sipping on his eleventh Martini of the morning.

"Are you coming back to Earth Odjy?"

"Yes, if they'll have me. There's nothing happening on Zenar with everyone gone. Not until the wedding next month anyway. I'm dancing for them, you know. Will you as well Sarah?"

"Ah, I don't know, I haven't thought about it."

"Of course you will. I'll arrange it."

They'd already been for a morning swim and were feeling jaded and at ease, a huge contrast to how they'd felt for the last few intense months.

Just then they heard a raucous from the direction of the hotel and the sound of gunshots.

They quickly got up and ran towards the tumult, as opposed to the other guests and staff, who were running away from it. The planet security were standing at the entrance to the hotel lobby, guns ready in their hands.

"What's happened?" Karl flashed his EI badge. Sarah couldn't believe he had it with him even on the beach.

The beings that lived on the Beach planet were an interesting kind. Half human and half fish, they would breathe like humans and walk with legs on the land, but when they entered the water, they could breathe like fish through gills in their neck, and their legs would fuse into a fishtail so they could swim. This ability came in quite handy when certain careless swimmers got into trouble.

The security officer spoke with a fish-like stammer, "Couple having a dispute, happens a lot, but when she decided to leave, this guy let off some shots into the roof, then pulled a knife on her. He's holding her over there, says he'll kill her and us if we go any closer. Got any ideas."

"Let me talk to him. Maybe he'll listen to a female, you know, less threatening." Sarah decided to make herself useful, seeing Karl always had to jump into the middle of a fray.
"Sure why not? It's your neck." The officer nodded over to where the offender held his girlfriend, and Sarah took that as permission to go ahead.
Karl started to object but she'd already walked out into the sight of the offender. Kahotep and Odjit had disappeared.
"Stop or I'll do it!" The man was obviously distraught, and held the knife alternatively pointing at Sarah and then back at the terrified girl he held in a headlock.
Sarah held up her hands to show she was not armed. "I'm not going to hurt you, I just want to talk to you. What do you think, can we just have a chat?"
The man looked at her suspiciously. "What do you want?"
"Is that your girlfriend?"
"Yeah, so what?"
"What's her name?"
"Miranda."
"You must love her a lot, huh?"
"Yeah but she cheated on me!" He pulled his arm tighter around her neck till she started gasping.
"How do you know?" Sarah thought it was a risky tack but it was worth a try.
"She was gone for ages this afternoon and last night I saw this guy comin' on to her at the restaurant."
"Really? And did Miranda talk to him?"
"Ah, no, she told him to nick off."
"So what makes you think she saw him today?"
"She was gone that's all." He began to soften his grip and looked down at the ground.
Sarah took a step forward and he held up the knife again.
"Did you ask her where she went today?" Sarah could see some of the security officers closing in out of the corner of her

eye.

"Yeah, she wouldn't tell me."

"So has she done this before, cheated on you?"

"No never."

"So do you think you could be wrong, you know, made a mistake about it, maybe?"

"Well, maybe." He was beginning to soften his grip again.

"Do you think you could let her go and we'll have a talk to her about it?"

It was then that Odjit stood up right behind him and put a gun to his head.

"You have two choices." She said, whispering menacingly into his ear. "You can put down the knife and you live. Or you can die right now. What's it going to be?"

The man dropped the knife and officers came from everywhere and pinned him down on the ground.

Sarah ran forward and caught the distraught girl before she fell to the floor as he let her go. The girl was then led away by more of the planets' staff.

The original officer they had spoken to walked up to Sarah.

"Well done." He seemed bored and was chewing on a toothpick. "Couldn't have done a better job myself. What's yer name, whereyer from?"

"Sarah Witnish from Earth."

"She's with me." Karl took her aside. "Do you think that was the wisest thing to do?"

He looked annoyed.

"Well you just plunge into everything, I was just following your lead." She was trying to sound confident, but she wasn't sure if he was buying it.

"Well, you're lucky you didn't get hurt. Well done." But he was frowning and didn't seem pleased.

Kahotep and Odjit walked up and joined them.

"Looks like someone's concerned." Odjit pinched Karl gently

on the arm. "Were you worried about her Karl? Looks to me like this girl can take care of herself." She was smiling wryly. "You both could have been hurt." Karl was still sulking.
Kaho decided to mimic him. "Yeah you got lucky. May not be so easy next time."
"Oh shut up, Kaho! You mean we should leave it to the men? You'all weren't doing the greatest job. You needed us to save the day!" She put her arm through Sarah's' and pulled her towards the bar. "We *female* heroes have some celebrating to do." And the two girls went off chuckling.

That night Karl had relented. He was a bit tipsy and walked Sarah to her door. "You were great today you know."
"I know." Sarah laughed. They'd reached her door. "Here I am."
She turned towards him to say goodnight but Karl kissed her slowly on the lips. She looked at him in surprise for a moment and then kissed him again. She then pulled him into her room and closed the door.

When she woke up in the morning he was gone. They were due back on Earth that day so she showered and got ready. They had breakfast as usual with Kaho and Odjit and neither mentioned the night before. After breakfast they made their way back to the ship and headed for home.

The holiday was over.

PRINCESS YASMINI

From the first time Prince Adabi of Zenar laid eyes on the beautiful white princess that he saw imprisoned in a bubble of snow, he had no doubt that he wanted to marry this girl. Her name turned out to be Princess Yasmini of the distant planet called Snow, and she was the sweetest and the smartest girl he had ever met.

Not only was she gracious in her beauty and power as a royal, she was the friend of everyone, from poor to rich and in between; she had the compassion that he felt was so lacking in his part of the world. For the longest time his people had become a spoilt nation, fat in their indulgence and ignorant in their seclusion.

But in the short time that she had been on his planet, she had become the darling of the people and had begun to open their eyes to the plight of the world that they sold their precious Krystal to. With the permission of the king and queen she had started an awareness campaign, highlighting the planets in the galaxy that did not fare as well as the blessed planet Zenar, and did not have any resources of their own. She showed the people how these races were completely dependant on their outside activities, and therefore remained poor, required to be away from family and friends for long periods just to survive. She held a public forum and then conducted a vote, and with the backing of the people formed an aid operation with research and distribution departments. She could not have done anything more to make the princes' heart swell with pride and admiration, and he was in awe of her.

But it was not only at home that the people clamoured for her attention, it seemed like every planet they visited wanted to get a glimpse of the snow white princess and they couldn't get enough of her. Since the announcement of their engagement, the couple were big news and they were mobbed by reporters and the public everywhere they went.

And now because of her impending nuptials into a wealthy dynasty, her obscure planet would now also become well known. But the prince thought that that was not necessarily a bad thing. They needed to increase their security anyway in light of the recent attack by Bosworth, and Richter was at this moment establishing a permanent team to dispense to the planet and oversee procedures.

The only downside to all this exposure was that since the announcement they never seemed to have any time alone. That's why they were looking forward to the stopover at the beach planet, even if it was very brief. So when they arrived they greeted their friends and then locked themselves away in their hotel room.

"Some time alone at last my future wife." He kissed her lips for a long time and moved his hands along her back down to her buttocks and then up again, rubbing her shoulders.

His face looked troubled and she could see it. She ran her hand over his forehead. "What's wrong my sweetheart, you look troubled?"

She always seemed to have a maturity much beyond her years but he knew she'd been through a lot on planet Bosworth, just like he had. He pulled her over to the balcony and they stared at the beautiful vista laid out in front of them, the wide open sea that stretched for miles to meet the horizon, the sound of the waves crashing onto the shore is all they could hear; the sea was busy within itself, it gave the impression that there was nothing else, it was unconcerned with the outside world. But Adabi knew better.

"You know when I was imprisoned on Bosworth I felt stupid

and helpless, I even thought that I might die. I berated myself for not doing more with my life or for others and I'd even put others in peril with my stupidity." His face was pained and she could feel his anguish. She realised he had not fully recovered from the ordeal.

"You can't possibly blame yourself. You know you'll always be a target, just like I am, it comes with the territory. We just have to live with it and be more careful." She ran her hand through his dark curls. They fascinated her because all the men and women on her planet had long strands of white, straight hair. He turned to look into her blue knowing eyes.

"I know. But I never got to tell you that as soon as I saw you in your bubble prison you inspired me. I knew you were something special. I couldn't stop thinking about you and in my desolation the thought that you were imprisoned too, kept me going and made me determined to survive. And now look at you. You're a marvel, you've done all these things on my planet and to think we could have both been killed, it just upsets me." He kissed her again and held her tightly.

"C'mon darling, that didn't happen. Now lets enjoy this short time we have alone okay?"

"Of course, I'm sorry. I just wanted to tell you that though that was the worst time of our lives, it made us find each other. That we had to go through that awful time but ultimately it was the best thing that ever happened to me. You're such a trooper. Come here, I'm going to ravish you!"

She giggled and ran off into the room but he caught her and pulled her onto the bed into a long, languishing kiss.

The first thing Adabi felt as he stepped off the ship on Snow, was the fierce bite of the freezing cold on his skin. Although he was shivering he was mesmerised by the extraordinary sight in front of him. The planet was a shining white that bedazzled the eyes, a sheet of soft snow to walk on and the soft fall of the snowflakes in the sky, falling like rain to the ground. He had never seen snow in his life and it surprised him. He took his glove off regardless of the cold and felt it, wet and dissolving as it met his warm skin.

"My goodness, it's fantastic!" He looked at Yasmini, her eyes were smiling proudly, a big grin on her face, delighted at his reaction.

"It's truly beautiful." He gave her a huge squeeze and took her hand.

"You don't feel the cold?" She wore the white flowing gown that seemed to be the uniform on her planet and he was concerned.

"I already told you, we don't feel temperature like you do. Now pay attention!" She squeezed his hand and pointed her gaze to the approaching welcoming committee. The heavy snow fall suddenly lightened and Adabi drew in his breath as he began to distinguish the shapes between the screen of white flakes.

Queen Yoroni was walking toward them, flanked on each side by an accompaniment of male and female guards. She walked on a path that was lit with a beam of light on each side and behind the lines stood white horses with men and women sitting alight them holding white trumpets. In an instant they lifted their instruments but instead of the loud noise that he would have heard on Zenar, a beautiful sweet melody began, and rose and fell in time to the soft wind that blew across the land. In unison the white horses lifted their heads in reply and an answering melody erupted from their mouths.

Queen Yoroni stopped still in front of the prince. His father and mother King Ptah and Queen Irisi, fell into place beside him and he looked at them in surprise. He didn't know they were going to be there. His mother smiled at him.

"We thought you might need some support." She turned her

gaze to the Queen standing in front of her.

"We formerly welcome the Royal Family of Zenar to the Planet Snow. We are pleased to receive the fiancé of our daughter Princess Yasmini and his family into our community. Welcome Prince Adabi, King Ptah and Queen Irisi of Zenar."

While Adabi expected a loud roar as would be the case on Zenar there was complete silence. The Queen then raised her arms and a great flutter of snow white doves flew up behind her and into the sky above. At this there was a soft murmur from the crowd watching, and the Queen lifted her arms again. Behind her a huge swarm of white butterflies flitted all around them and then flew away intermingling with the falling snow.

Queen Yoroni raised her arms and eyes to the sky. "Thank you Great Lord of the Snow. You have restored our planet to its former glory. Blessed be all who walk upon it." And with that she turned around and began walking back down the lit pathway.

Adabi could not see where it led through the snow but Yasmini tugged on his hand and they all followed.

The eerie melody began again, and the horses lifted their heads beside them as they walked by, until the huge form of a clear glass building appeared before them. The queen walked through the glass but Adabi hesitated expecting it to be solid but Yasmini tugged his arm and pulled him through. The glass seemed to be a liquid that felt like water when you passed through it. He looked behind to see if his parents were following inside, but they laughed when they saw him.

Inside, the formality was over and his mother came up and hugged him.

"How are you my boy?"

"Good thank you mother. But what are you doing here?"

"Why should you have all the fun? We were invited by the queen of course. Besides this way the formalities are out of the way in one go."

His father greeted him. "How are you son?" His embrace was full of warmth.

"Good thank you father. I'm so glad you decided to make the trip. Are you feeling alright?" His parents had not left Zenar for many years and he knew his father would be slightly apprehensive.

"Fine son, it was time. We came with Richter so all went well."

"How long have you been here?"

"Just a few days, we left Zenar soon after you. It's lovely isn't it, the snow I mean?"

"It's incredible. Just like their princess." He put his arm across Yasminis' shoulders and pulled her close to him.

Queen Yoroni dismissed her guard and joined their conversation.

"How was your holiday children? You must have needed it after all the attention you've been receiving. You're all over the world news. How are you coping?" She kissed her daughter and Adabi on both cheeks.

"We're fine mum, now can we go? I want to show Adabi around."

"Of course, we'll see you at dinner. Five o'clock in the private dining room." She walked up to Adabi and took both his hands in hers. "You have made us all so happy. Bless you." She let his hands go again. "Now go." She waved them away smiling at her daughter.

She turned to the king and queen. "You must be so proud of him. He is such a strong courageous soul, I can see it."

"Yes we are." The queen looked in the direction the couple had gone. "But he feels things you know. I do worry." She turned back and laughed. "Just being a mum."

Then Queen Yoroni led them away to prepare the feast that would be tonights welcoming dinner.

GAULE

Sarah looked up to see Karl standing at the door of her office looking at her.

"Gosh, you startled me." Not only had she not heard him come in, it was uncharacteristic of him to be nonchalant at work.

She walked past him with a concerned look. "Be careful, you'll get us caught."

He followed close behind her so that she could feel his breath on her neck. "What, by looking at you?"

"We have a meeting you know, you're making us late."

"What, by talking to you?"

She chuckled as she increased her pace to put some distance between them. They had agreed to keep their romance secret, especially at work, they did not want it to compromise any standing they had in the light of their superiors, but Sarah thought Karl was sometimes too complacent. She felt sure others were looking at them and guessing that something was going on. Although Karl liked to stir her paranoia and annoy her, keeping it a secret was just a bit of fun for both of them and it gave their flirtation a cheeky edge.

The only one who had guessed at their tryst was Odjit and she had returned home to Zenar to help her relatives prepare for the royal wedding in one months time, so there was no chance of their secret coming out.

But as soon as they walked into David Spencer's office they concentrated on the business at hand. And that business was Bosworth.

"Good morning team." David addressed the four EI agents. Tamara and Dominic were already seated.

"We have had some disturbing news while the two of you have been busy." He glanced at Sarah and Karl. "Tamara will fill you in." He sat down at his desk.

Tamara remained seated but her low heavy accent held a tinge of unrest. "We have located Bosworth but unfortunately there are complications with extraditing him back here for trial. He has formed an alliance with the planet Gaule. Gaule was once a sister planet of Earth, populated initially by a small group of natives who departed two centuries ago from a time when Earth was still divided into separate countries. Even then they were a troublesome group, not wanting to assimilate into the general Earth community, as is the case now. They have been one of the small portion of planets that have so far refused to join the galaxy council. We also have reason to believe they have resumed their uranium enrichment program, which as you now is illegal across all galaxies. They have declared in an official statement that Bosworth obtained contracts for mining on Earth that was originally sold to them long ago by another group who left Earth, a people called the Arabs, original owners of the desert areas concerned. Further they intend to appeal the decision against Bosworth for the right to mine the Krystal find on Earth." Tamara sipped a glass of water, giving the others a chance to absorb the information.

David stood up and continued. "Thank you, Tamara. The Krystal mine has been found to be considerable. We of course will fight the appeal and win. A review has been set for September so we have a couple of months to prepare our case. In the meantime we have all been invited to the wedding on Zenar which we will attend as a team. Any questions? Good." He continued before anyone could respond. "Tamara and Dominic please continue preparing for the court case. Karl and Sarah I need you to research the extent of the weapons armament on Gaule. You will enter undercover as new apprentices in the renowned school of cooking in the capital city. This is an ongoing assignment requiring a duration of an eighteen week stay, you will leave the planet to attend the wedding only, and then return. Good work, all of you. The two of you will be happy to know that this assignment compliments the current state of your relationship. See you at the wedding."

It was the first time Sarah had heard David Spencer chuckle and it took her a moment to realise that he was referring to her dalliance with Karl. She walked out of his office quickly, a soft blush appearing on her face.

Gaule was a sumptuous planet of rich old architecture and a world bursting with the love of all things edible. The planet had rebuilt its original infrastructure that it had had on Earth, at times transporting whole buildings across space, such as the famous cathedral of Notre Dame, an historic gateway called the Arc de Triomphe and a famous tower called the Eiffel. It was a planet steeped in a small part of the past history of the planet Earth and Sarah revelled in its old world charm.

As David had said, it was renowned as the cooking capital of the galaxy and through generations of expert chefs had set up cooking schools that were the envy of other planets and exported culinary geniuses all over the galaxy. They were in demand from the best resort planets to the highest paying private employers, and as celebrity chefs across the satellite television stations.

Sarah and Karl were enrolled in the distinguished Ecole le Cordon Bleu in the capital city named Paris, the most prestigious cooking school in the galaxy. Their cover was as a young couple with the intention of commencing new careers and it was the ideal background for the two agents to revel in their new-found love affair. They were housed in a small apartment in the Montparnasse district only a short walking distance from the school. It was a pretty little flat, perfect for

the portrayal of a typical pair of students embarking on a new
career path.

In between classes they immersed themselves in the
plethora of cafés and restaurants the city had to offer and
enjoyed the rich cultural heritage of a timeless atmosphere of
luscious food and heady love. It seemed their were couples
everywhere and Paris was known as the city of love.

But it was not all play. Karl would have to find a way to
infiltrate the planets intelligence agency and determine the
size of their illegal nuclear arsenal, if they had one. And he
had a plan. But to Sarah's' frustration he would not share it
with her. They always had these conversations in a secluded
part of one of the many centuries old parks, where they were
sure no one could overhear them. Today they were in the
Jardin des Plantes, where they had just strolled through the
natural history museum. They were standing underneath a
row of enormous hundred year old plane trees. Karl stopped
to look up at the beast that dwarfed him.

"It's just better that you don't know. It's dangerous and I don't
want you involved in
this part."

"I thought we were in this together. I'm supposed to help, you
know."

"You are helping, you're my cover. But the rest I go alone. Two
people are more noticeable and anyway I'll be in places you
can't go. Support me on this would you, please?" He pulled
her toward him. Just as quickly he let her go again. "But make
sure you're ready if we have to leave quickly. Ok?" His brow
suddenly furrowed and she realised that he meant that as a
possibility.

"Okay."

"That's my girl."

Sarah didn't know it but while they had been placed in the

cooking program together as a couple, EI had also placed Karl into a training program of fighter pilots for Gaules' elite air squadron. He was to be employed as an instructor on a training mission, and because he spoke fluent French, their native language on Gaule, and his training as a fighter pilot on Earth, he slipped easily into the role.

After he reported to the Gaule Air Force, he was required to remain on base, so Sarah had to cover for him at the cooking school, which she found more difficult to do as the days went by.

"Is your boyfriend still sick?" The head chefs voice seemed to boom and echo in the hollow kitchen.

"Yes, I'm sorry, I'm afraid his stomach just hasn't acclimatised to the beautiful rich food of Gaule." She hoped that a little flattery would diffuse the awkward situation. It
seemed to soften the chef and he lowered his voice.

"Well I'm afraid that if he misses any more classes he cannot gain his certificate, tell him that."

"Yes, sir, I will."

The truth was that Karl had been gone now for two weeks with no word, and she had begun to get worried. She decided to do a bit of research on her computer and try to find him. She looked into defence news for the planet Gaule and it wasn't long before she came across an article with Karl s' picture. 'Decorated military air force instructor Lieutenant Terry Lakin to conduct training mission on Gaule.'

"So that's where he is!" Sarah thought.

It was going to be a long sixteen weeks on her own as the cooking school finished early in the afternoon, so she decided to get a job. She emailed one of the EI secretaries. She needed a second identity on Gaule.

Sarah walked into the Gaule Defence Force headquarters with her new resume in her hand. She had an appointment with the administration manager on the tenth floor for an IT position within the building. She was not nervous; she was determined that she would show Karl she could be more than a seat minder. She had worked on her French before they arrived on the planet, and after two weeks it came naturally to her.

"Miss. Perrot? Please follow me." The administration manager was a slim, tall, elegant woman, her navy suit typical of the polished appearance of the Gaule workforce.

"Please sit down." She motioned to a chair. "Your reputation precedes you. I must admit I was most surprised when I read your profile. You will fit in well here, welcome."

"Just like that?" Sarah tried to hide her surprise.

"We could not let a person with such experience slip through our fingers. Let me show you to your office."

Sarah would have to take the EI secretary to lunch.

The Gaule Defence Force was a twenty four hour machine so the administration bosses saw no problem with Sarah, or Camille Perrot, as she was known, choosing to work in the evening hours. She wasn't sure how much time she had because she had not heard any word from Karl, she supposed it was too dangerous for him to make any contact that could be detected easily inside the planet; so she proceeded to locate the main computer on the top floor straight away. The top floor could not be accessed without a biometric pass so she would have to take a hostage when the time came. The thought of that did make her nervous, but there was a first time for every agent and this would be hers. The security of her planet depended on it.

As an IT employee in the defence force building Sarah was

given certain basic codes and passwords to enable her to do her job. She set about using one of these information streams to try to contact Karl. She quickly learnt how to locate and track anyone that entered the country and one night she developed a secure personal line and contacted Karl s computer when she knew he would be off duty.

Karl saw a signal coming into his laptop. He was surprised as no one except from EI knew his contact information. He touched the screen to receive it.

'Karl, it's me Sarah. Don't ask questions but I'm working in Defence Headquarters just outside of Paris. I will have access to their main computer only once then I'll have to get out of here. What do you need to know?"

Karl was surprised to learn that she also had another mission but was quick to realise the potential this had to make his job easier.

"I need the locations of nuclear development facilities. Before you go in let me get everything ready. Call me again in two days."

Karl closed his computer. He hoped EI knew what they were doing.

"It's me. Are you ready?"

"Yes. And be ready to leave tomorrow night."

"I'll relay the information at 1200 hours."

"And Sarah?"

"Yes?"

"Be careful."

She wished he hadn't said that. She wanted to concentrate on the task not think about the danger. She put it from her mind and walked to the elevator that would take her up to the top floor. She felt in her pocket the lipstick case that contained a paralysing nerve gas injected with a needle the size of a hair-shaft. She waited for the guard she had chosen as the closest to her height and weight to come by. Although their routes were randomly changed every night, she knew he always came to the cafeteria on this floor around this time.

He rounded the corner and greeted her with a nod. She jabbed him in the neck as he strode past and he fell to the floor immediately. She dragged him into the elevator and put first his hand into the security detector and then pulled his eye up to the screen.

"Which floor would you like?" The elevator asked.

Sarah placed a small device behind the guards neck and spoke through it so that it stimulated his vocal chords.

"Twenty four." She then pushed a sleeping pill down his throat.

The elevator doors opened and Sarah sped out towards the main computer room. She had spent hours memorising the floor plan. The corridor was empty and she slipped silently into the room and sat down at a computer desk. She knew she didn't have long and began typing codes into the screen. It wasn't long before she was given access and sent the location data straight to Karl s' laptop.

She pulled out her chair and made for the elevator. The guard slept peacefully slumped on the floor.

"Ground floor."

Sarah made her way to the departure terminal to wait for Karl so they could leave the planet, never to return.

Sarah felt the buzz of her mobile before she heard the noise of an aircraft overhead.

"Jump in!" Karl was hovering above her in a foreign fighter jet. He lowered it to the ground next to her and as soon as she scrambled in, he took off. It was then she noticed some aircraft coming towards them in the distance.

"Hang on!" Karl whipped them into hyperdrive and they shot up out of the atmosphere and into space in a matter of seconds. The fighters pursuing them took aim and fired but

Karl was quick to avoid the fire. He zoomed away from the planet but the Gaule air force stopped at the planets outer zone.

"They've stopped."

"Yes, I thought they would. They don't know if I have reinforcements out here. It wouldn't be wise for them to follow."

"You stole a Gaule jet fighter?!"

"Well I didn't have time to change aircraft did I?"

Sarah looked whimsically back. "What about my cooking certificate?"

Karl looked at her and realised she was serious. "We just got away with our lives and you're worried about your certificate?" He shook his head smiling. He was beginning to wonder which one of them was more fearless.

"You stole a Gaule jet fighter?!" David Spencer spoke to Karl as he and Sarah walked into his office. "Now where am I supposed to hide that thing?"

Sarah had found out that just before Karl picked her up to leave Gaule, that he had destroyed all three of the uranium enrichment plants on the planet with their own jet fighter. But over the news networks there was no mention of any sabotage, only that there had been an industrial accident on Gaule that was now contained.

"You both did well. But Sarah, before you decide to take on the top security military establishment of another planet could you give me a heads up first?"

"You mean you didn't know?" Karl looked at David and then at Sarah in surprise.

"Did I mention Karl, that Sarah has done a bit of hacking in her spare time before she came to work with us?"

"You know about that?" Sarah looked embarrassed.

Karl lifted his leg and swept his arm in a large circle to

exaggerate clicking his fingers. "I knew it!"

David changed the subject. "Well, you're back just in time for a royal wedding. Lets go."

THE ROYAL WEDDING

The planet Zenar was in a frenzy. The royal wedding between their only prince, Prince Adabi, and his beautiful fiancé, Princess Yasmini of Snow, was scheduled to take place in two days time.

The streets and buildings were lined with tributes to the couple, flags representing the two planets were everywhere and the population was descending on the capital city.

But for a kilometre around the royal palace, the area was out of bounds to the public until the wedding. The couple had left the arrangements to the family, and the two Queens, Irisi and Yoroni, were overseeing every detail. Not only was there all the decoration to take care of, the guest quarters for the Snow people would be regenerated, and within the kilometre radius around the palace, the climate would be acclimatised to suit them. The official duration of the celebration was to be one week but everyone knew Zenar would celebrate for much longer.

The two queens had decided on a colour scheme of gold and white, representing the two countries. Queen Yoroni had brought with her on her return, white doves and white butterflies, as they were plentiful on her planet, to be released straight after the ceremony. She would also supply white horses for the transport commencing at the outskirts of the city and proceeding to the royal chapel. Queen Irisi would take care of all the food implementation such as the gold crockery and cutlery, and the rest of the decorations would be a mixture of both colours. The white roses that had been ordered from the Flower planet would be decorated with gold ribbon; the white chairs and tables would be inlaid with pure gold, as would the white carriages that the wedding party would travel in. But the one thing the two mothers spent the most time designing was the wedding dress. No-one, not even the bride, was allowed to see the dress before the day and its location was also kept a strict secret, the milliners clandestine entrance into the planet undetected. The traders in fine materials presented their wares in private receptions to the two finicky women. The finest silk was brought in from the traditional harvesters in the Asian sector; rare pink diamonds and the highest clarity white diamonds were presented from Ricar, the diamond planet; and the subtlest of pure gold lining was imported from the planet of gold, Eusina Eopa.

Everything was going to plan and though security to the planet was at the highest level it could be, the galaxy was buzzing with the news of the impending nuptials.

Adabi and Yasmini had been kept apart for the last month before the wedding, as was customary on Zenar. Adabi had left Snow and returned to Zenar with his parents only days after the ceremony of welcome, as his parents were anxious to return so that they could finalise the arrangements with only three weeks to go before the appointed day of the ceremony.

He was missing his fiancé terribly. With the two queens overseeing all aspects of the day, and his father and Richter taking care of security and the accommodation of guests, Adabi was left with little to do. He milled around listlessly and for once it was he that was annoying Kahotep. He would have a restless sleep and be up early in the morning, but not know what to do with himself.

He barged into Kaho's room, who had already started celebrating the wedding early, partying outside the castle perimeter with the visiting girls from the various regions of the planet.

" Kaho wake up!"

"Ohh, not again, do you know what time I went to sleep? An hour ago!" He turned over and put his head under the pillow.
"Cmon Kaho, I'm bored." Adabi sat down on his bed dejectedly.
"Come back later, Cos, we'll talk."
Five minutes later Kaho looked up but Adabi was still sitting on the end of his bed.
Kaho sat up. "Ok, what's up?"
" What do you mean?"
"Something's been bugging you for days, now what is it?"
"I told you, I'm bored. Yasmini's not here and the two mothers have taken over the wedding, I've got nothing to do."
" That's not it, I know you better than you know yourself, now out with it."
Adabi blurted out his words quickly. "What if I'm not good enough for her."
Kaho shook his head in disbelief but realised straight away his best friend was serious and needed reassurance. " Are you crazy? You're the prince!"
"Stop that. You know, she's so industrious and well, just so smart."
"Look dabby, you're the smartest guy I know. And more than that, she's crazy about you. It's just nerves that's all. Of course it's a big deal, but you two are made for each other! And I'd tell you if it wasn't true."
" Really?"
" Really. Now listen, your dad's given me a job, what time is it?"
"Aahh, six o'clock."
" What? Dammit dab, you owe me. Now c'mon, you're gonna help me. Give me that robe and I'll have a quick shower."
Kahotep had been given the job of envoy to all the diplomats that had invitations to the wedding and were now on Zenar waiting for the ceremony to start the next day. It was the day

before the wedding and Adabi was a bunch of nerves so he thought he'd give the prince something to put his mind to.

When all the guests were sitting at lunch in the great hall, Kahotep stood up and tapped his glass with a spoon to get their attention. Dominic sat beside him and Adabi was seated on his other side after being overrun with congratulations from the attending patrons.

"Attention everyone! On behalf of Prince Adabi, we thank you all for being here!" He raised his glass. "To Prince Adabi and his bride!"

"Hear, hear!" There was a sustained tinkering of crystal.

Kahotep held his glass up again. "We have a treat for you all today. Prince Adabi has volunteered to give you a tour of the best sights around the planet. To Prince Adabi!"

"Hear, hear." Another loud tinkering.

"What?" Adabi looked surprised.

Kahotep took a big mouthful of drink and winked at Dominic before both men stood to leave. "That'll keep you busy, Cos."

"Hey where are you going?"

"I'm showing Dominic some of the rarer sights of our gorgeous planet."

At home on Snow, Yasmini was restless and three weeks suddenly seemed like a long time. She was finding the change in climates difficult and only enhanced the feelings of distance that was between her and Adabi. The fact that her mother was away on the planet Zenar arranging everything for her did not help her feelings of agitation. But she was being fussed over by her five sisters, and as the youngest, and the only one who was not yet married, they wanted her to look her best for her wedding on the world stage. And although she felt unsettled at home, she could not resist the girls constant excitement and chatter. Now there was only one week to go but it seemed like the hours would never pass.

"We have a surprise for you!" The girls ran into the room and jumped on her bed.

"Not another facial or massage or makeup experiment! I'll have no skin left by the time you're finished with me. Look it's all red from too many creams and lotions." She held a mirror up to her face to show them.

"No, better!"

"Come in!"

Sarah was dragged through the door by one of the sisters.

"Look who's here!"

Yasmini jumped up in delight. "Sarah, you're here! Thank you, my sisters are driving me crazy. Maybe you can get them to leave me alone." She squeezed her tightly.

"Of course, I am. But I'm going to drive you crazy too!" They all started screaming in glee and dancing around the room.

Sarah shivered. "Now where's a heater?"

Finally the day had arrived and the crowds were allowed into the restricted zone. It seemed the whole population of Zenar was lining the streets leading up to the holy chapel where the wedding would take place, and they jostled each other in delight to get a glimpse of the procession.

A layer of synthetic snow thickly covered the ground along the main avenue and synthetic snow machines on each side regularly pumped out huge amounts of snowflakes at intervals that coincided with the ebbs and flows of the dulcet music. A lot of the people had never seen snow before and they marvelled at its beauty as it fell on their skin and hair. The EI team had been allocated exclusive seats to witness the ceremony but they like everyone else, lined the streets to enjoy the parade.

The procession began with the military band of Zenar, a glorious line of soldiers in gold uniform, the heralding trumpets in front exclaiming loudly and proudly the significance of the day. They were followed by the distinguished dancing ladies in their brightly coloured costumes signifying the successful harvests of the centuries old planet. Next came various musicians in between representations of various gods, the sun god, god of the moons, god of music, god of love, god of the sea and many others.

But the ones that the crowd were waiting for, were the beautiful white chariots commandeered by majestic white horses. And they finally came. There were four carriages all together. The first carriage carried the King and Queen, the proud parents of the groom, waving at the delighted crowd from the open top. The second carriage carried Queen Yoroni and three of the sisters, waving and shouting at the thrilled onlookers lining the sides of the road; and the third carriage, this time enclosed, carried the lovely bride, Princess Yasmini, and the remaining two bridesmaids, her sisters.

The procession made its way to the entrance to the holy cathedral and dropped their passengers one by one.

The dazzling bride dressed all in white, stepped out of the carriage with the bridesmaids attending to her long white train. The ruffled veil covered her face but the spectators could see the happy glow she exhumed. Although she was a foreigner, they knew her well already; she had given herself over to them and she had captured their hearts. She took a moment to turn and wave before she entered the church. The crowd roared and then looked towards the televising screens to witness the occasion they'd all been waiting for.

As Princess Yasmini walked behind her mother, Queen Yoroni, into the magnificent temple where she was to be married, a great cheer echoed behind her and a collective gasp of approval met her from within. She was a vision to behold, her dress an exquisite masterpiece, the diamonds reflecting brilliantly in the golden light; and she herself, who seemed to walk with an air of certainty and purpose.

Adabi saw his princess enter and his heart swelled with pride. He could hear the amazement in the oohs and aahs of his witnesses but they could possibly understand the love that he had for the girl who was taking the long walk toward him down the aisle. He remembered the first time he had seen her, and recalled the longing he felt when their eyes met. He now felt that longing again, and as she came to stand beside him, he turned towards the priest with an assurance in his heart that he'd never felt before. He repeated the priests words with conviction and finally he could lift the veil and kiss the lips of the girl that was always going to be his bride. And in doing so he felt the pieces of his life all come together into the right order. The story was complete.

The clapping and the cheering followed them out into the frenzied masses, and the pure white doves and butterflies flew off into the golden expanse of sky. They laughed and danced for days and the golden glow of Zenar radiated into space.

THE END.